BLOODY MAYHEM DOWN SOUTH

Treasure Coast Mayhem

TRAYVON D. JACKSON

Good2Go Publishing

Bloody Mayhem Down South
Written by Trayvon D. Jackson
Cover design: Davida Baldwin
Typesetter: Mychea
ISBN: 978-1-943686-40-7

Copyright ©2016 Good2Go Publishing
Published 2016 by Good2Go Publishing
7311 W. Glass Lane • Laveen, AZ 85339
www.good2gopublishing.com
https://twitter.com/good2gobooks
G2G@good2gopublishing.com
www.facebook.com/good2gopublishing
www.instagram.com/good2gopublishing

All rights reserved. No part of this book may be reproduced without written permission, except for brief quotations to books and critical reviews. This story is a work of fiction. Characters, businesses, places, and events and incidents are either the product of the author's imagination or used in a fictitious manner. Any resemblance to actual persons, living or dead, is purely coincidental.

Dedication

This book is dedicated to a fallen soldier, someone who taught me the game when I was brave enough to venture into the jungle. In loving memory. We miss you, cuzo. RIP Cents Daddy.

Acknowledgements

My first thanks goes to God for once again making it possible to reach my dream. Next goes to the Good2go Team for keeping me on my game. I would like to thank my assistant, Latoya M. Moye, for all her help and support she's been giving me. I also want to thank her sidekicks Keke, DeeDee, and Meka for keeping Latoya company. To my mother—Frankie Mae Jackson—stay strong, Momma, because this is just the beginning. It gets greater later. To my beloved siblings—Shada Keys, Jamar Young, Clarissa Young, Johnesha Miley, Jashanti Miley, and Johnny Miley, Jr.—my love is always with y'all. To my nephew and nieces, I love y'all, and Uncle will be home soon to hang with all of y'all. I would like to give a shout out to my enormous family tree: Queens, Ruckers, Weavers, Broomfields, Jacksons, Mileys, and Wilkins. Free Lee and Leon Barnette! And to my fans, continue to rock with the boy, and I promise to keep my best coming.

"Planning takes calculation, and calculation takes patience."

~ *Trayvon D. Jackson*

BLOODY MAYHEM DOWN SOUTH

Treasure Coast Mayhem

TRAYVON D. JACKSON

Chapter One

Florida, DOC
Martin County

*T*wenty *minutes until count clear, and I'll be out of this muthafuckin' hell hole. No more dealing' with these pussy-ass, low-self-esteem rednecks and hillbilly, imbecile Negros. Damn! I did this shit, and I did it like a soldier too. I've been pacing this cell since the lights came on at 4:00 a.m. for breakfast—a breakfast I dared not eat on my last day.*

"So, Real when you gonna shoot the money to Chucky?" Kentucky asked his pacing cellmate, who was anxiously preparing himself for his release after five years down for possession of a firearm by a convicted felon.

Real abruptly stopped at the cell's door and then told Kentucky for the umpteenth time, "Like I told you, I'ma handle that ASAP."

Real was definitely a man of his word—the strongest weapon a man had in prison—and was better a dead man without it. He was leaving Kentucky the one hundred dollars that the Department of Corrections provided inmates upon their release. Real didn't need the shit, and Kentucky was his best friend.

"Man, I really appreciate that man. Without you it's gonna be eerie, Real. Damn! I can't believe you're actually going home, nigga!" Kentucky spoke while sitting on his bottom bunk reviewing a manuscript that he had written for a book.

Real and Kentucky were each other's equal at five foot seven and 200 pounds, solid from their team workouts and solid protein diets. They were both committed too. The only distinction between them was the color of their skin. Real was a swarthy, chocolate-complexioned nigga. Kentucky, on the other hand, was a pale-ass cold-blooded white boy from Scottsville, Kentucky, who came from a lethal hood called Landmark. Kentucky was the realest white boy that Real had ever met in prison, with a heart of a lion—a lion that would never see the streets again unless he succeeded in a great escape.

"Brah, without me, you would still be straight. I told you I'ma take care of you and Chucky, my nigga," Real reminded him.

"Man, you be cool out there," Kentucky retorted, laying down his manuscript and becoming attentive to Real.

"Get that money, follow through with your plan, brah, and you'll be that nigga in no time," Kentucky said.

"Hell yeah, brah! You know I'ma follow through, and you, my nigga, keep these bustas out ya game room," Real warned.

"Because Florida CIs are—"

"Everywhere," both Real and Kentucky said in unison while giving each other their unique handshake.

They both heard the dormitory door slam, and knew that it was an officer entering the wing to conduct a head count.

"Sit up on your bunks, inmates!" a female guard ordered all inmates in their assigned cells.

"Oh shit! That's my baby!" Kentucky exclaimed as he rushed to the cell's door to get a view of the most toothsome female CO at Martin Correctional.

Her name was Ms. Queen, a petite caramel-skinned young lady who was a relative of Real's. Real shook his head at Kentucky's obsession with his cousin. Despite Queen being Real's cousin, no inmate other than Kentucky knew, and she was strictly about her business and played by the rules of the book.

"When she write yo' ass up for stalkin', don't be cryin' about 'I need someone to send me something in the hole,'" Real warned Kentucky.

At Martin Correctional, it was rare for an inmate to get thrown into the hole for reckless eyeballing a CO, especially a female CO.

"Man, I ain't going to no hole, because I'm not stupid to get caught," Kentucky said while lusting over Queen, who was on her way to the top tier to conduct count, giving him an exclusive view of her nice firm ass.

"Here she comes!" Kentucky said as he quickly returned to his bunk to avoid a count violation.

Kentucky saw that Real stayed in his spot near the toilet, adamant about not hopping on his top bunk.

"Nigga, you better get on your bunk!" Kentucky warned in a whispered shout.

"What's she going to do to me, Kentucky, write me up?" Real retorted, and then briefly laughed.

Looking at himself in the mirror over the sink, admiring his elegance while simultaneously brushing his hair with a no-handle brush, he could taste the freedom on his tongue. He had a head full of beehive-designed waves, of which he proudly took care. When he heard Queen's footsteps halt in front of the cell door, Real turned around and saw her writing down her last count on a little notepad. He then looked into her eyes as she looked into the cell.

"Inmate Jermaine Wilkins," she briefly paused, indecisive of whether she should yell at Real for being off his bunk in violation of count procedures. But she decided against it and continued, "You're to report to the sally port once count is clear, with all of your property, and prepare for end of sentence."

With nothing more to say, CO Queen moved on to continue her count.

"It's official now, nigga!" Kentucky exclaimed, soaking in the reality along with Real.

"Hell yeah!" Real retorted.

"My nigga! It's over with," Kentucky said as he leaped from his bunk and embraced his best friend, with tears in the wells of his eyes.

"Don't worry, my nigga. I got you," Real reminded his true friend.

"Clear count on the compound inmates. It is now clear count!" proclaimed the master control CO over the loud PA system.

* * *

Shamoney sat in the parking lot of Martin Correctional Prison, waiting on his brother Real to come through the prison gates that had confined his eldest brother for five long years. He was elated and eager to see his role model break free of his chains. Emanating from his car system on a respective low volume was 2Pac's hit "Rear View" while he puffed on a phat dro blunt.

Shamoney was the second oldest of the rest of his siblings. He was a year younger than Real, who was twenty-three, and towered over him about an inch and a half. Unlike Real, Shamoney was a red-skinned pretty boy, who was stupid with the gun play and fooled a lot of his enemies.

Damn, brah about to get out here. I know he 'bout to wreck shop with me, Shamoney thought while smoothing the waves in his head with his hands.

Shamoney was deep in the dope game, which was no different than any other nigga in the dope game in Martin County all the way to St. Lucie County. He was selling dope for the notorious Haitian Black, the infamous drug lord who the feds desperately wanted but could not locate.

At twenty-two years, old, Shamoney thought that the figures he was seeing and lavishness was cream and honey. He was unaware of the plan his brother Real had in mind. It was a plan that if it succeeded, subsequently would promise them a meal ticket out of the hood and make them superior over all hoods.

When Shamoney looked up and saw his brother coming through the gates in the fitted outfit he had bought Real to come home in, he quickly emerged from the conspicuous '88 candy-red-coated Chevy Caprice on twenty-eight-inch Savini rims.

"God damn, nigga! Ma told me that yo' ass was big as hell, but not like Hogan, nigga!" Shamoney exclaimed in high elation, overwrought as he embraced his brother.

"What's good, nigga?" Real asked his little brother, glad to see him after five years, since the state had prohibited him from seeing Shamoney because of his record.

"Man, you looking good, nigga."

"Shit! You looking better than me," Real retorted, pointing at Shamoney's tricked-out Chevy Caprice.

"I'm just eating, nigga. You wasn't missing out. Where do you think all yo' canteen came from?" Shamoney enlightened Real, who knew that his brother Shamoney was in the dope game.

"Where's Johnny?" Real inquired about his youngest brother.

"That nigga on a mission. We'll catch up with him," Shamoney spoke.

"I see," Real retorted.

"Man, let's get you away from this shit hole!" Shamoney said as he strutted off toward his Chevy.

Once inside, Real took in the comfortable opulence of Shamoney's Chevy. The nigga had televisions everywhere in the dashboard. His red suede seats and cherry wood grain set off the car. Real observed that his brother had some serious taste. As they peeled out of the parking lot, Real saw the recreation yard that was swarming with inmates for the first recreation call.

I ain't never coming back to this shit. I'll hold court in the streets before I do, Real thought.

"Man, what's up? Do you want to stop in the hood before we head out west to see Ma?" Shamoney asked, speaking of their hood across the tracks a mile down the road from the prison.

"Yeah, let's see what the swamp looking like," Real retorted.

"Here, light this up and relax," Shamoney recommended, tossing Real a lighter and a phat dro blunt to get his mind level with his cloud nine.

Shamoney blasted the 2Pac hit while accelerating the loud dual exhaust pipes on his Chevy. Real inhaled the dro blunt with veteran lungs. Despite being incarcerated, Real and Kentucky smoked weed on the regular. So, he had no low tolerance when smoking the blunt.

Damn! I'm out that shit. I can't wait to see the hood, my nigga. Only if they knew shit was about to get real, nigga, Real thought.

* * *

"Hell no! Nigga, let her go!" shouted out a bad bitch named Lala who was wielding a two-by-four as she charged her baby daddy, Joc, who was shielding his mistress from Lala's hood beatdown.

"Lala, chill the fuck out, bitch!"

"Bitch nigga! I got yo bitch!" Lala screamed and then vigorously struck Joc in the back with the two-by-four.

Whack! Whack!

"Muthafucka! I got yo' bitch!" Lala continued attempting to hit Joc again, but she was restrained by her girl, Pimp.

"Come on, Lala. That bitch ain't worth it. Let's go," Pimp said as she held onto her and pleaded for Lala to leave the situation alone.

Lala was twenty-six years old and stood five six, with her Coke bottle frame and gorgeous brown skin. She remained furious and adamant. Everybody in the hood knew that her patience with Joc's infidelity would run slim.

"This ho ain't got enough heart to give me one," Lala yelled.

"Bitch, ain't nobody 'bout to fight you over no dick out here. Grow up, child!" the mistress, Keshia, screamed.

She was a redbone, old-school cougar who had innumerable freckles on her face, which accentuated her beauty. The street at Jake's corner store on the main strip, at 5th Street and MLK Boulevard, was growing increasingly crowded. Keshia's sisters were there to support her, but Lala had a vicious clique behind her, ready to pounce if any of them decided to get stupid.

"Fuck you, ho! You wasn't talking sense when you picked up my nigga's phone. Anybody knows that's a cardinal move. Now be a woman and get this ass," Lala yelled as she found an opening when Joc purposely moved to the side and rushed Keshia with swinging arms and closed fists.

When Real and Shamoney pulled up to the crowded store with a blasting system, they both saw Lala demolishing Keshia.

"That Lala's fine ass, brah?" Real asked Shamoney.

"Yeah, that's Lala. Still giving these hos all the hell they want. I bet you any kind of money they fighting over Joc's crazy ass." Shamoney sighed as he parked in the dirt which served as a parking lot on the side of Jake's store.

When Real and Shamoney stepped out of the Chevy, a couple of niggas jumped in to break up the fight.

"Looks like the swamp ain't aged one bit," Real said.

"Hell no! Same old Booker Park, brah," Shamoney retorted, calling the swamp by its government name.

"That you, Real?" one of Real's childhood homies named Lunatic exclaimed as he ran toward him.

"My muthafuckin' nigga!" Lunatic yelled as he bear-hugged him.

The commotion from the fight instantly died, and the new focus was Real back in the swamp. Finding a good time to get back at Joc's infidelity, Lala rushed Real and gave him a hug to welcome him home. Real was her past, and she knew that at the moment, Joc was staring daggers at her back.

"Damn! You've grown up, Real!" Lala exclaimed with lust-filled eyes, breathless from the fight.

Lala had her hair pulled back into a ponytail and was wearing skin-tight short-shorts and a sports bra. She was gorgeous.

"Shit! Look at you. You've grown into—"

"She's taken, my nigga. So, slow ya nuts down. She being a tramp right now," Joc said with slight sternness in his voice.

Lala rolled her eyes nonchalantly and then turned to Joc. "Fuck you, dog-ass nigga! Go see 'bout yo skank-ass bitch!" Lala said spitefully.

"I am," Joc sternly said while staring down Lala.

"Listen, Joc. Whatever y'all got going on, keep that shit out of my face," Real warned, as he was ready to make his first example that he was still that nigga—ruthless and untamed.

"Man, everything cool, homie," Joc copped duces. "Don't take nothing the wrong way. The beef is with her, not you."

"Lala's my friend."

"And no nigga gonna get between our friendship," Lala signed for Real.

"Man, brah, let's go see Jake's old ass," Lunatic said as he pulled Real away from Lala and Joc.

"Joc, don't bring no shit to my brother 'cause we straight whackin', nigga," Shamoney said to Joc while simultaneously pulling up his black T-shirt and revealing his Glock .40 tucked in his waist.

Joc's silence conveyed to Shamoney that he got the picture as Shamoney strutted off to catch up with his brother, who was still dapping up niggas from the hood.

Lunatic, Shamoney, and Real walked into Jake's store to see Real's favorite old-school of the swamp. Jake's store was an old, boarded-up house from the front that had a wooden swinging door with a dirty screen as a window.

When the trio entered, Jake was behind the counter, engrossed with a television program and sitting in his comfortable La-Z-Boy chair with his hands locked behind his head. The inside was dimly lit from the old light bulbs that dangled from the ceiling.

"Jake, guess who done jumped out the pen?" Lunatic's loud voice boomed, breaking Jake's attention from the fishing program he was watching.

When Jake looked over the counter, he abruptly leaped out of his chair. "Muthafuckin' Real!" he exclaimed as he dashed from behind the counter to embrace one of his favorite little niggas.

Jake hugged Real like he was one of his many sons. Seeing Real's eighteen golds sparkle ominously, Shamoney knew that his brother was enjoying every moment of his new freedom.

"Man, you've grown and looking like your daddy, nigga!" Jake said. He was a close friend of Real and Shamoney's father, who was serving a life sentence in a federal penitentiary in Orlando for a bank robbery gone bad.

"I see you still runnin' the shack," Real said, causing everyone to erupt into laughter.

"Yeah, the old man still runnin' the shack!" Jake responded, scratching the gray stubble on his face.

Real noticed the gray hairs dominating Jakes head and realized just how fast life moved for everyone.

Damn ol' boy getting old fo' real, Real thought.

"This shit would have been lit up, my nigga!" said Lunatic, who stood five eights and weighed 205 pounds. He had dark brown skin, lengthy dreadlocks, and a mouth full of gold, just like near damn everyone from the swamp, including ol' man Jake, who stood five eight, weighed 185 pounds, and was black as night.

"That's how I wanted it to be. Don't worry. I have to surprise a lot of my niggas," Real said as an understatement, which everyone missed. *If only they knew!* Real thought.

* * *

Damn! Real is home and lookin' fine as hell. That nigga Joc was hating his ass off. I gotta get that nigga on speed dial and see if he could make this pussy squirt like he did when we were younger, Lala thought.

"Girl, is you okay? I swear, ever since you seen Real's ass, you've been spaced the fuck out!" Pimp said to Lala, her head bitch in charge.

There were five girls in the Ms. Gorgeous clique. They stuck together through whatever and had a credit card scam on lock.

Mookie, Nut-Nut, and Luscious were the other three Ms. Gorgeouses, and they were all chilling at Lala's crib on 4th Street like every night while playing cards, smoking, and drinking.

Mookie and Luscious were the chocolates of the clique, while Pimp, Nut-Nut, and Lala were on the dark brown side. And like their name, they were all gorgeous.

"She thinkin' how she goin' to fuck Real without Joc killin' her ass!" Mookie said, exhaling dro smoke from her mouth while passing the blunt to Pimp at the kitchen table.

"Whatever! Y'all hos don't know what y'all talking about," Lala said, blushing as she walked into her spacious kitchen.

"Oh yeah?" Nut-Nut said, with a naughty smirk on her face.

"Y'all ease up off Lala. Shit! We all had a nigga fresh out of the joint on our gotta fuck 'em list!" Luscious exclaimed, causing everyone to erupt into laughter.

"I know. That's right, bitch!" Pimp said, giving Luscious a high five.

Lala looked on and rolled her eyes.

"You ask me, girl, fuck him on the low so that Joc's ass don't kill you," Pimp said.

"Fuck Joc! If I wanted to fuck Real, I sure ain't worried 'bout how he feel 'bout it. He fucking Keshia," Lala said as she sucked her teeth. "He better not come in my face on no ho shit, or I'm gonna squeeze on that nigga," Lala retorted, squeezing the trigger on an imaginary gun, which caused everyone to laugh.

"So, who you think he gonna be fuckin' with?" Pimp inquired.

"Me, if I want him, but backtrackin' only gets a bitch caught up, just like the rules," Lala stated, reciting one of the clique's rules.

Fuck it. I'ma be his bitch! Lala thought, desperately craving Real's affection and body like she once had.

Chapter Two

Real awoke the next morning in a guest room at Shamoney's opulent four-bedroom home that he shared with his wife, Chantele, who was a gorgeous swimsuit model who had helped Shamoney stay under the fed's radar. Despite her dislike of Shamoney's dealings in the dope game, she loved him and would do anything for him. Her net worth was a million dollars, but was certain to increase in due time.

Real turned to his left and saw the gorgeous brunette named Kimberly, who was a friend of Chantele's. She enjoyed the pleasure of being the first to fuck Real, and she did everything in her pussy power to break him.

"Good morning, handsome," Kimberly said in her Mexican and British accent.

"I'm coolin' it," Real said, scratching his stubbly chin. "What 'bout you?" he added as he grabbed her five foot three, 125-pound frame into an embrace.

"I'm lovely," she said, smiling brightly before she quickly immersed beneath the covers and took Real's erect dick into her mouth.

"Damn, ma!" Real purred from her pleasure as she sucked his dick slowly while moaning as she worked up to a rapid pace.

As she sucked his dick, Real's thoughts went back to Lala. He recognized how much she had grown and how gorgeous she still was. He couldn't believe that she was now a mother of a pretty little girl fathered by Joc. It took Real a lot of self-control not to pounce on Joc the day before. When Joc tried to calm him down, Real knew that Joc wouldn't last in his wrath.

Nigga, I'll fuck yo' bitch in front of you if I want! Real thought.

"Mmmm!" Kimberly moaned as she continued to suck the shit out of Real's dick.

Not wanting to spoil her chances of feeling Real inside her wet, sultry pussy, she came up and straddled Real before slowly sliding down his dick.

"Yes!" she exhaled, biting on her bottom lip as she began to ride him slowly.

"Damn! This pussy is grippin', shorty," Real exclaimed.

Despite seeing Kimberly, who was a straight dime piece diva, Real still thought strongly of Lala from the swamp.

Shamoney had put him up on everything that was going on in the streets. He knew of the ballers and bitches that were getting paid. What disturbed Real was that every hustler came back connected to Haitian Black, a nigga who had come out of nowhere and regulated the Treasure Coast. Even his brother Shamoney was connected to Black.

No man is their own man, Real thought conclusively.

Real wasn't down for serving for no man but himself, and he was about to wake up Black's million-dollar drug-lord ass with a surprising left hook. Real was determined to take over Black's turf and regulate by all means. It was a plan that he had thoroughly thought about while in prison, and he was about to make it a reality now that he was home.

"Uhhhh, Real! I'm coming!" Kimberly moaned out in ecstasy as she came to her orgasm.

Real artistically reversed her, balling her little ass into a missionary cannon ball and vigorously pounding away at her tight pussy.

"Uhhh! Shit! Real! Uhh!" she shouted as he slammed his dick into her excessively wet pussy, just like he was about to unmercifully drop lead into any nigga who didn't get down with his regulation.

* * *

"Hurry up, pussy-ass Arab, and empty that register before I give yo' ass something to hesitate about!" Lunatic screamed at the trembling man behind the 7-Eleven counter in Port St. Lucie.

Lunatic had been on a robbing spree, holding up convenience stores early in the mornings. The stores were randomly picked, so the police had not yet discovered the three men in masks.

"Bitch, I said hurry up!" Lunatic barked again, growing very impatient by the ticking seconds.

"Man, I got something to make his ass hurry up!" T-Gutta yelled as he turned his Glock .40 on one of the store clerks who was lying on the ground.

Boom! Boom! Boom!

"Okay! Okay! Okay! Everything man, take it!" the Arab screamed in panic after seeing T-Gutta blow the brains out of his sister-in-law's head.

T-Gutta was a slim, six-foot-tall red-skinned twenty-one-year-old who was from Martin County, from a hood called East Stuart. He and Lunatic were codefendants on a lot of robberies, and both were made for each other.

Lunatic gathered the money and then prepared to leave the store, when he noticed they were running over on time. On most occasions, the duo was in and out in under two minutes. Hearing the sirens approaching, Lunatic aimed at the Arab's chest and then fired.

Boom! Boom! Boom! Boom! Boom!

"Let's go!" Lunatic shouted, grabbing the bag of money as he stormed out the front door with T-Gutta on his heels.

They both made the getaway to where their third compadre awaited them behind the wheel of a stolen Dodge Ram pickup. His name was Alleycat, a superb getaway driver.

As soon as the duo hopped inside, St. Lucie County sheriff cruisers swarmed the 7-Eleven from a back entrance.

"Roll, Cat!" Lunatic yelled to Alleycat, who smashed on the gas and merged into traffic on US Highway 1 and initiated a chase. The police cruisers immediately pursued the black Dodge Ram, simultaneously calling in the stolen plate numbers.

"Shit!" Lunatic exclaimed.

Out of all the damn times they had hit stores and successfully gotten away, a minute too late had caused them to be in the trouble they were in now. Fortunately for them, Alleycat was an artistic driver when it came to eluding the police in times like this. He swiftly maneuvered through traffic, running red lights at intersections, and caused a wreck behind him.

Damn! That nigga sho' knows how to handle that wheel! Lunatic thought as he held onto the support bar above his head.

"Shoot 'em off, so I can duck us off!" Alleycat shouted.

Without any reluctance, Lunatic dropped his window and grabbed a MAC-10 that was resting on the passenger floor for backup. He racked it and then sat out the window. While holding on to the support bar with his right hand, he simultaneously fired at the pursing police cruisers, causing them to swerve and wreck. T-Gutta pulled back the Ram's sliding back window and stuck his twin Glock .40s out and participated in the fusillade. Every police cruiser that came in view was knocked off by the duo.

Alleycat made a right onto Port St. Lucie Boulevard, going west, and vigorously accelerated through more traffic lights.

When the trio made it to Bayshore Boulevard, Alleycat turned right and then abruptly made a U-turn, causing Lunatic to almost lose control, but he held onto the bar like a raging bull's ropes.

"We about to dump!" Alleycat said as he turned into a Publix store parking lot, upsetting the pursuing cruisers who were trapped in the wreckage behind them.

The trio quickly exited the Ram truck and carjacked the first occupied vehicle they saw. Alleycat pulled the old white woman from the driver's seat of the tan Dodge Grand Caravan and blew her brains from her head.

Boom! Boom!

Alleycat put the Caravan in drive and inconspicuously drove away from the plaza, in the opposite direction. He quickly found the first I-95 ramp and traveled southeast until he was in Martin County again.

Damn! That was close, Lunatic thought.

Selling dope for Black was unprofitable when every man was doing the same thing. He wasn't fortunate like a handful of niggas, who had become prestigious dope boys and were seeing big numbers in the dope game.

Robbing had become his main hustle. Although it was petty change, it was money in his pockets that the dope game wasn't bringing in for any of his compadres.

I think it's time for us to hit a bank, Lunatic thought.

* * *

When Shamoney and Real pulled up to their mother's beautiful home in Port St. Lucie about thirty minutes west of Shamoney's crib, they saw that family had already arrived for Real's welcome home cookout.

"Ma done popped off early, I see," Real stated.

When he emerged from the conspicuous Chevy and smelled the BBQ cooking on the grill, he was ready to get his grub on.

Their mother had married a devoted Christian man named Migerle. He was a Haitian man and had loved their mother, Michele, since childhood. When their father caught life in the fed, Michele had moved on and given her life to Christ, ultimately giving up on the street niggas.

"Hey, Cousin Real, it's good to see you home," Real and Shamoney's fine-ass cousin Tiffany, exclaimed giving Real a hug.

Damn! If she wasn't family, I'd try her all day, Real thought.

"Thanks, Cuz. I'm home now," Real retorted.

"Stay home, okay?" Tiffany said to Real as she looked over at Shamoney.

"What's up, big money? Let Cuz get a couple dollars?" she asked Shamoney, who had become the bread and milk winner to the family.

Before Shamoney could pull out his wad, Real stopped him.

"I got it, Cuz. What you need?" Real asked Tiffany after pulling out his wad of cash he had accumulated from all the niggas who broke him off.

"No, Cuzo, I can't! You just came home. I should be giving yo' ass something!" Tiffany spoke.

"I'm cool here, Cuz," Real said, placing three $100 bills in her hands as he walked off.

"Thanks, Cuzo," Tiffany said.

"Welcome," Real turned around and said, then proceeded into the house past little kids who had no idea who he was.

When Real stepped inside his mom's luxurious home, his little sister, Precious, who was fifteen years old, ran up to him from the crowded den of kids. She hugged her brother tightly, obviously glad to see him.

"Jermaine, I'm so glad you're home."

"What's up, lil sis?" Real asked Precious, who was growing into a model too damn fast and developing like a mango.

"Daddy called, and he wanted to talk to you!" Precious exclaimed.

"Yeah, nigga, you missed pops. He's calling back at five o'clock," Real's baby brother, Johnny, said.

Johnny was twenty years old, a mixed breed, and the only child who had a different father than Real, Shamoney, and Precious. Real's mother and father had briefly separated, and during that time Michele slept with an Asian man, from whom she got pregnant. Despite Johnny never knowing his biological father, who instantly disowned him, Real's father, Rob Bass, took in Johnny as his own.

"Where's Ma at?" Real asked Johnny.

"She's in the back helping out Migerle. You know that Haitian can't cook!" Johnny exclaimed.

Johnny stood five foot six, weighed 165 pounds, and had strong Asian features. People called him Chyna Man on some occasions because of his slanted eyes.

He looked like a straight pretty boy, but he was a straight killer who was quick to slang iron on any nigga that looked like a threat.

Fort Pierce City, or Killa County, in St. Lucie County was known as the murder capital, and it was Johnny's stomping grounds.

"So we going to the club tonight?" he asked.

"Y'all need to be going to church instead of a club, mister," Michele sternly said to Johnny as she walked in from helping Migerle and met all her kids in the living room.

"Ma, I do go to church," Johnny answered.

"Try coming tonight, tomorrow, and on Wednesday. Migerle preaches good," Michele said. "Shada, when you coming back?"

"Ma, you know I don't do no church now. I only came that one time because of your birthday," Shamoney retorted and then stormed off past his mother and walked outside where the family was gathered.

"Son, don't get out here and get caught up in them streets again. Neither of your brothers has experienced prison, and by the grace of God, I hope they never have to. Jermaine, get you a job and find you a good woman."

Real was vaguely listening to his mom, but deep down inside, he knew that he was far from letting go of the streets. Not a day had passed for him in prison that he hadn't thought of coming back to the streets to regulate.

"Do you hear me, son?" Michele asked Real, whose mind was attentive somewhere else.

He was deep in the streets, and now he was about to make his name ring like bells.

"Yeah, man. I hear you," Real said as he looked over at Johnny and Precious, who saw the nonchalance in his eyes.

"Come, your Auntie Betty wants to see you and Grandmother Dot is here too," Michele said as she grabbed Real by his arm and led him out back.

* * *

Killa County (Ft. Pierce City)

"So this is how we gonna play, huh, T-Bo?" Haitian Pat asked the bloody-faced man from 23rd Street.

Pat was a ruthless Haitian and right-hand man to Haitian Black of the Haitian mafia. He was the most feared Haitian on the Treasure Coast. When he came for his money, he came with an entourage of other vicious Haitian men. Pat stood five eight, weighed 195 pounds, and had a menacing swarthy complexion. One look at him was the epitome of death.

Tonight he had finally caught up with T-Bo, a dope boy who had just turned eighteen, who was in serious debt with the Haitian mafia. He was caught slipping, leaving the Elk's Club with his bitch. He had nowhere to run when Pat's five Haitian men boxed him in by his car in the parking lot. His bitch was dome-checked by one of the men's Glock .40s. T-Bo was knocked out, snatched up, and kidnapped.

When he awoke, it was the most pain he had ever endured in his life. Pat continued to mercilessly torture T-Bo by cutting off his nose with a hand saw. Naked in a chair, bound by heavy-duty rope, he was feeble and begging to die quickly.

"You'd rather die for $40,000?" Pat said in a heavy Haitian accent. "Big Chub, hand me the bolt cutters," Pat ordered his 300-pound right-hand man, who stood five nine, with a swarthy complexion.

Big Cub wasted no time walking over and grabbing a bolt cutter from the garage wall.

"Mmmm, mmmm!" T-Bo tried speaking behind the duct tape.

"So you know where my money's at?" Pat asked as Big Chub handed him the freshly oiled cutter.

Pat vigorously snatched off the duct tape, allowing T-Bo a chance to better sign his fate.

"Speak!" Pat barked at T-Bo, who was wincing in pain.

"Man, I can explain everything. These niggas robbed me for the bricks, Pat. So I've been trying to catch them."

"What niggas? Who robbed you," Pat asked.

"Some niggas from Martin County in East Stuart. I don't know all of them, but I know one from beef, Pat," T-Bo explained.

"Who is this nigga you got beef with?" Pat asked as he lifted up T-Bo's chin with the bolt cutter.

T-Bo looked up at Pat with his one open eye, unable to use the other because it was closed shut.

"His name is Shamoney," T-Bo lied.

Pat began to laugh hysterically, causing perplexity to fall upon T-Bo. He had no idea how stupid he had just made himself look.

"So, Shamoney is the man you beef with, and he robbed you?" Pat asked him.

"Yeah, he robbed me, man! Agghhhhh!" T-Bo screamed out in pain as Pat rammed the bolt cutter through his good eye, and twisted it. "Aggghhhh, Lord!"

"Nigga, you take me for a dummy, huh?" Pat shouted as he then clamped the bolt cutter around T-Bo's dick and snapped it off in one clean snap.

"Nooo! Lord!"

"Finish him, Big Chub!" Pat ordered, throwing the bloody bolt cutter to the ground as he stormed away.

Boom! Boom!

As Pat walked outside the garage side door, Big Chub stuck the shotgun into T-Bo's mouth after hitting him in his chest. He then squeezed the trigger twice more.

Boom! Boom!

When Big Chub caught up with Pat inside the Suburban, Pat had just gotten off the phone with Black.

"Big Chub, call Shamoney and tell him to meet me in the morning at the trap in Lake Park," Pat ordered Big Chub as they made their way back to Palm Beach County.

Chapter Three

Shamoney had just pulled off from one of Black's trap houses after dropping off eighteen ounces of cocaine to one of his female clients, Tamara, when he received the call he had been waiting for.

"Youngin', what it is, my nigga!" Shamoney answered as he slowly cruised through the hood in East Stuart, where the cocaine moved faster than any other drug that a hustler pushed in the trap game.

Shamoney had just flooded the main strip of Tarpon with more of Black's addictive product.

"When will you be ready, soldier?" T-Zoe asked Shamoney, who was a known hit man for the Haitian Mafia.

Bitch-ass nigga ain't no soldier over here. It's boss, nigga! Shamoney wanted to tell T-Zoe, who was his equal in age.

He hated T-Zoe with a passion, and once even got a chance to rough him up, but Pat had saved the nigga's day. Shamoney looked at his gold Rolex with scintillating blue and green diamonds, and saw that it was shortly after 3:00 p.m.

I gotta go pick up Real from the DMV in an hour. Then maybe I can bring him to the gambling house on Tarpon and come back in an hour flat, Shamoney thought about how he would evade Real to handle business with Pat.

"I'm ready, but I gotta handle something before I come that way, so I'ma hit you back in an hour when I'm on my way," Shamoney told T-Zoe.

"Alright, soldier. I'll tell ya, brah, what time is it?" T-Zoe said before disconnecting the phone.

As Shamoney slowed at a stop sign, he saw a Stuart cruiser pull in behind him. He made a left and then another quick left on Bahama Street with the police still behind him.

Cracka wants to pull over a nigga, Shamoney thought as he came to another stop sign on Bahama. *Good thing I'm clean. No K-9 unit hitting.*

"What the fuck!" Shamoney yelled at seeing the police lights twirling red and blue, informing him to pull over.

"Shit!" he exclaimed as he removed his Glock .19 from his waist and tossed it under his seat.

Shamoney wasn't driving the conspicuous Chevy that day, so he had no idea why the police officer had pulled him over in his luxurious all-black .745. He calmly pulled over to the side and let down the window.

No smoke. Nothing! Why is this cracka pulling me over? he thought.

Shamoney watched the slim, six foot four redneck walk up with his hand resting on his service revolver.

"Sir, what is the problem?" Shamoney asked.

"The problem is that your tag says St. Lucie County and you're driving in a high crime and drug neighborhood," the officer said as he spit a glob of tobacco juice from his mouth.

"And your point is? I have family here," Shamoney retorted.

"Do you have any warrants?" the officer asked, avoiding answering Shamoney.

"Do you have probable cause?" Shamoney retorted sarcastically.

"No, but I need to see your license," the officer said with an impish smirk on his face.

Shamoney noticed a K-9 unit pull up behind the police cruiser, and smiled and shook his head.

"Don't you think it's time for the dog to go lay down," Shamoney said impertinently.

"Yeah, do you have something for him to hit, boy?" the officer asked furtively, dropping a bag of cocaine outside Shamoney's driver's side door when he reached over to grab the registration out of the glove compartment.

"If that dog hits anything on this car, I'll suck his dick!"

"Step out of the car, boy. We have reason to believe that you're concealing drugs in this car after seeing you leave a known drug area," the officer ordered.

"Man, are you kidding me?" Shamoney exclaimed, heated. He became more furious when he saw more cruisers pull up to the scene. "All y'all for a traffic stop?" Shamoney said as he opened the door and stepped out, never seeing the small baggie of crack on the ground.

"Sir, please turn around so I can check you for weapons."

"What we have, Jed? Is he dirty?" another redneck officer asked, with more tobacco in his mouth than his partner.

The officer was walking up while putting on gloves to help assist with the search.

"We're about to see now. He says if he's dirty, he'll suck Buddy's dick."

"Wow, I'm sure my dog will love that. Ain't that right, Buddy?" the owner of the K-9 unit exclaimed, getting two barks from his dog.

When the officer opened the back door to his squad car, Buddy the German shepherd exited. He had been on the force for nine years.

Woof! Woof! Woof!

Buddy barked as he ran to Shamoney and then sat down in front of him and the baggie.

Woof! Woof! Woof!

Muthafucka! These crackas done set me up! Shamoney concluded when he saw what Buddy was sitting next to.

"Damn, Buddy, what have we found?" the K-9 officer exclaimed as he knelt down and picked up the small baggie of crack.

"Man, that's not mine!"

"Shut up, liar!" Officer Jed said as he pushed Shamoney over the hood of his car, kicking his legs apart and then handcuffing him.

"Man, that's not my shit!" Shamoney yelled.

"Yeah, yeah, we know! Be quiet. You're under arrest, and you have the right to remain silent."

"Oh shit! He has a burner, because I know you're a convicted felon," the K-9 unit officer said as he held up the Glock .19.

Shit! Shit! Shit! Shamoney thought, knowing that this case could definitely land him in prison, a place he had been dodging for years now.

* * *

Real had been calling Shamoney's phone for the past two hours and getting no answer from him. When Johnny pulled up in a Tahoe Chevy truck on twenty-eight-inch Forgiato rims instead of Shamoney, Real knew that something was amiss.

"What's up, lil brah?" Real asked Johnny as he climbed inside his brother's truck.

"Shamoney just got popped. He's been in booking for two hours now. Crackas won't give him no bond until he sees a judge," Johnny explained.

"Damn! What did they get him with?" Real asked.

"Nothing too major except the gun."

"Gun! He got caught with a burner?" Real exclaimed, knowing how Martin County was the wrong place to get caught with an illegal firearm.

"Yeah, that's what I told him," Johnny added.

"So where you got to be at? Did you get yo' license?" Johnny asked Real as they pulled out of the DMV and into traffic.

"Hell yeah, nigga! I got it," Real exclaimed, showing off his driver's license that he had just obtained.

"Well now it's time to go get you a whip," Johnny said as he merged onto I-95 northbound and accelerated.

"Yeah, I guess so, lil brah!" Real agreed.

He had more than $50,000 to his name that Johnny and Shamoney had put together to put in his pocket. But that still wasn't enough to hold him down when the free life was moving so fast.

I gotta get on my grind, and I mean soon, Real thought as he listened to Rick Ross's "Port of Miami" emanating from Johnny's thunderous system.

Almost there, my nigga almost! Just a couple more days, Real thought.

* * *

Man, I can't believe these muthafuckas done tried me with that bitch-ass move! Shamoney thought furiously.

He was still sitting in the holding cell at Martin County Jail waiting for his booking process to complete. He'd talked to his wife, Chantele, and told her to be in court first thing in the morning with a bail bondsman. He didn't care how preposterously the judge would set his bail, because he was sure that he had the 10 percent and collateral to move him.

"These crackas can't stop no getting-money-ass nigga," Shamoney said to himself out of frustration.

Despite the self-encouragement, Shamoney was seriously worried about the firearm charge, because he knew how strict the Martin County system was against them. He was in the middle of the tri-county's Murderville, where unsolved murders were in the highs. So every nigga with a gun charge, the judges were definitely throwing the book at them.

Damn! I can't let these crackas convict me on no gun case, man. I'm getting too much money right now to fall short, Shamoney thought.

At his home that he shared with Chantele, he had a total of $150,000 in his name from pushing for Black, who had the entire coast on lockdown. He knew that with all the work (kilos) that had touched his hands, he was supposed to be sitting on a million or better. But he was like every other penny hustler getting what he could. He was just fortunate to be on a different level from a lot of the other hustlers. He was connected to the mafia through Pat, and that was the only reason Shamoney was the man in Martin County.

"Damn, I gotta get out of this shit!" Shamoney persistently stressed.

Chapter Four

Miami, Florida
Miami Gardens

As Black sat at his desk in his office in his mansion, he thought about all the corruption that was going on around him in Miami. There were murders committed every day between the two mafias of the Haitian culture. For years he had been at war with the Zo'pound gang in Miami, who wore black and white bandanas as opposed to the Haitian mafia who wore the original Haitian flag bandanas and who remained adamant about respecting the Haitian mafia that Black had raised from the ground up. Black had finally had enough and was anxiously waiting for darkness to fall because the head man in the Zo'pound gang, who thought that his whereabouts were furtive, would pay dearly with his life tonight.

Black was an old, swarthy, old-school forty-seven-year-old veteran of the game. He had been killing niggas for ages and sparing no loved ones, ensuing in chilly scenes from his wrath. Black was a strong believer in voodooism and was protected by the powers of them—the same as his number one nemesis, Polo.

Mr. Polo, I'll have you just like the rest of them who tried desperately removing me from this game. The FBI can't even fuck with me. What makes you think that you can keep up, Mr. Polo? Black thought, refusing to acknowledge that Polo was just as powerful as he was.

Black checked the time on his costly Hublot watch, and no longer than a minute later, two knocks came at his door.

"Come in!" Black permitted the visitor.

When the door opened, Pat strutted inside by himself dressed in all-black attire and gun holsters hanging with two Glock .40s between his armpits. Black looked at his thirty-seven-year-old compadre and knew that Pat was ready to go at Polo as much as he was anxious to go himself. But he couldn't, and only Black and Polo knew why neither of them could die by the hands of the other.

"What's up, Haitian?" Pat said to Black as he took a seat on the plush sofa in front of Black's desk.

Black slid back into his plush chair, threw his legs on top of the ornate, oak wood desk, and crossed his arms.

"You tell me, son," Black retorted back to Pat in Creole.

"Polo is still at the Marriott, and all his men are under the scope as we speak. Do you persist on bringing him out alive instead—"

"I need him alive, Pat," Black interrupted, "so that he can look the man he's been at war with in the eyes," he said while pointing his index finger at his eyes.

Pat understood the principle well and nodded his head in agreement. Together he and Pat had conquered the streets in the tri-county area and had been expanding their reach further toward central Florida. Like the Haitian mafia, Polo was a vicious Haitian who had Zo'pound in every county from Miami to Orlando. With every means to take out Black from the game, the two old Gs' beef had evolved from a cutthroat move that Polo did to Black when they were running compadres. The two of them once had a brotherly bond, until Black walked in on Polo fucking his ex-wife. He tried killing Black in the process of escaping, leaving Black's wife bullet-riddled in bed.

Polo was a wise man with a lot of grimy stunts at forty-eight years old. He was a high-yellow-skinned Haitian who stood precisely five foot eight and weighed 215 pounds. He was solid and equal to his nemesis, Black. Both Black and Pat knew that going after Polo would not be feasible due to the high security he kept around him and, unbeknownst to Pat, the power of voodooism that Polo highly possessed.

"We'll bring him alive, Black, if that's what you want," Pat stated.

"So what's good with the tri-area, Pat?" Black asked, changing the subject to a business inquiry.

Pat cleared his throat and sat up straight on the sofa. "It's better than we've ever expected," he said in Creole.

"Good, good, good," Black responded in Creole as he then continued to speak to Pat in their native language.

"I know that you have everything under control, Pat. Just keep your head in the game, son, and keep Big Chub occupied," Black spoke of his three-hundred-pound nephew who was Pat's right-hand man.

Black had brought Big Chub from Haiti precisely six years ago to assist Pat with the mafia.

"I will, trust me. We are holding the tri-area down like some real Zoes, Black," Pat confidently exclaimed.

"And how is Gina doing?" Black inquired of Pat's wife.

"She's doing good," Pat answered, shaking his head. "She's due in two months."

He was gladsome to be a father of his first son among three pretty girls.

"Will he be a junior?" Black asked.

"Yes indeed! My boy will be a junior—"

Pat stopped in mid-sentence when Black's phone chimed in. Black paused Pat with one finger.

"Hello," Black spoke in Creole.

"He's back," the caller said as he disconnected the phone.

Black looked over at Pat, and from the look on Black's face, it was evident to Pat that it was show time.

"Pat, let's move. Word is he's back," Black informed.

With nothing else needed to be said, Pa leaped from the sofa while making a call on his iPhone as he stormed out of Black's office. When he was gone, all Black could do was pray that the gods would be with him.

"Pat, bring Polo—and bring him fast," Black exclaimed as he then prayed for his compadre's safety and ultimate sacrifice.

* * *

Precisely forty-five minutes later, at 12:20 a.m., Pat pulled up to the Marriott hotel on South Beach, two Suburbans deep.

He didn't have his daily entourage that he kept close by in the tri-county, but these men were just as vicious as his entourage, and he knew them all thoroughly. Inside was their infiltrator who had purposely gotten close enough to Polo's vicinity and was a big help in making it possible for the Haitian mafia to finally locate Polo.

"Pierre, I need you to keep a visual on the lobby and main road. Bo-Bo, I need you to do the same from the side and back court," Pat ordered through his ear piece.

"That muthafucka is on the tenth floor. The only way he's coming out of that bitch is if he's Superman and thinks he can fly, Haitian," Pat's driver, Pierre, exclaimed. "And I doubt that nigga can fly!"

"Y'all ready for this shit?" Pat asked his team through his ear piece.

"Hell yeah!" Bo-Bo retorted in the second SUV.

"Let's roll, nigga!" a Haitian named P-Zoe said from the backseat behind Pat while racking his AK-47.

Pat pulled down his ski mask and racked his AK-47 rifle for assurance.

"Let's go! Move!" Pat ordered, and then exited the SUV simultaneously with all of his men and bum-rushed the entrance of the Marriott and initiated a deadly fusillade.

Chop! Chop! Chop! Chop!

Pat rapidly sprayed at the front desk, taking down four employees. He then took the flight of stairs to avoid the elevators for entrapment. Behind him were six men all prepared to war it out. And that's exactly what came upon them. Polo's men were in the stairway on the sixth floor and surprised them with a fusillade.

Tat! Tat! Tat! Tat!

Polo's men quickly caught two of Pat's men, but failed to hold their own as Pat nailed them from an angle.

"Come on! Let's go!" Pat shouted as they unexpectedly took the sixth floor as a change of plans.

They hopped on an elevator with four men and headed to the tenth floor.

"Bo-Bo, are we clear?" Pat asked through his ear piece to see what the outside looked like.

"Clear," Bo-Bo answered.

"Pierre, are we clear?"

"Clear," Pierre said as the elevator doors opened on the tenth floor, and Pat met the infiltrator who had killed off Polo's guarding men.

"What's up, Sunni?" Pat said to the chubby old-school Haitian who had worked his way up to Polo's trust before finally betraying him.

"He's still in the room!" Sunni informed Pat.

"Good job, Sunni."

"Here's the room key," Sunni said as he handed Pat the access card to suite 104B.

"Thanks," Pat retorted impishly as he then turned his AK-47 on Sunni and took him down.

"You cut one, you'll cut us all, Haitian!" Pat exclaimed as he stood over Sunni's dead body and fired twice more into his face.

Chop! Chop!

"That's for Black Haitian. We knew we couldn't trust you," Pat said as he made a dash to the suite.

Nowhere to run, Pat thought.

When he got to the door of suite 104B, he quickly swiped the key card and waited for the green light to appear. He then vigorously kicked in the door while meticulously stepping to the side. The four men with him swarmed the suite as he followed behind. Polo was nowhere to be found in the living room or kitchen. When Pat and his men came to the closed bedroom door, they knew that Polo had boxed himself in. Pat smiled, smelling victory while breathing heavily from running up the flight of stairs and his adrenaline rushing.

"It's over, Polo!" Pat shouted as he kicked in the bedroom door.

When he rushed into the room, Pat found him on the bed lifeless with his throat cut from ear to ear.

"What the fuck!" Pat screamed in panic and perplexity as he stared at the dead man on the bed—who wasn't Polo, but a man who strongly resembled him.

Pat had no clue that it was the work of voodoo staring at him.

"Let's go!" Pat yelled, sensing a setup.

"Pierre, are we clear?" Pat screamed into his ear piece while running from the site toward the elevator. "Pierre, are we clear?" he asked, again getting no response.

"Bo-Bo, is it clear?" Pat called out to Bo-Bo as he and his men took the elevator down.

Bo-Bo didn't respond either.

Not being ingenuous, Pat knew that he and his men were walking on eggshells and possibly a death trap when the doors opened. As they entered the lobby, the place was a wreckage. Sirens were closing in on them. Pat and his men ran to the SUV, where they found Pierre slouched over the steering wheel, obviously dead.

"Shit!" Pat shouted as he pulled back Pierre and saw that his neck was cut from ear to ear, just like the man upstairs who strongly resembled Polo.

"Damn it, man!" Pat shouted as he pulled Pierre's body from the driver's seat onto the ground and hopped into the seat himself.

Once all his men were inside, Pat started the SUV and then pulled out of the parking lot the moment Miami Metro Police swarmed the hotel, which was filled with shaken bystanders and a body count murder scene.

"Bo-Bo!" Pat called out again for his lookout, but got no answer.

Pat knew beyond a doubt that whoever had killed Pierre killed Bo-Bo too.

* * *

"I can't believe this shit, Pat!" Black shouted in rage after hearing Pat give him the rundown on the fiasco of getting Polo.

The gods misled me! Why? Black thought. "Someone's talking, and it's more than Sunni, Pat," Black quickly concluded.

He saw the vision and the infiltrator giving up Polo, and yet with so much corroboration he had still failed.

Pat sat on the edge of Black's desk, completely engrossed in bewilderment. He understood nothing of the works of voodooism, and Black hadn't explained to him that he was at war with a more powerful man than he had been led to believe. Pat only understood the turf war and not the voodoo war.

"He knew that we were coming, so he set up a lookalike inside the hotel and pulled one over on Sunni. All we knew was that Sunni said he was in the suite. But we never knew how close Polo allowed Sunni to get to him," Black explained.

What Black was insinuating sounded convincing to Pat, but he still had his skeptical concerns.

"Why not kill Sunni himself?" Pat asked.

"Because, Pat, he knew that we would take Sunni ourselves. What man could trust an infiltrator? That's like sticking yo' hand in a bag that you know has a snake inside," Black explained while rubbing his salt-and-pepper hair.

"If there—" Black stopped short of speaking when his iPhone rang. "Hello?" Black answered the unrecognized number.

"I lost a bet. Guess what it was, Black?" the irrefutable voice of Polo asked.

How the fuck did he get this number? Black thought.

"And what is that, my old friend?" Black asked in feigned surprise, as if he wasn't surprised that Polo had managed to get his number.

Pat had no clue who Black was referring to as an old friend, but the tone in Black's voice prompted Pat to give a look of wonder.

"I lost my money because I told someone that you would have been peeped. How weak your surroundings are. I used to watch you, Black. How could you possibly think that it would be that easy to bring wrath down on me?" Polo spoke and then began to laugh hysterically.

"Come out of hiding, pussy-ass nigga, and give it to me like a man, Polo!" Black screamed in rage.

"Of course I will, Black. When I catch you by the hands of yourself, we'll have our day, Haitian. Until then, don't self-destruct. How do you think I knew that you would be coming?" Polo said as he disconnected the phone.

"Pierre and Bo-Bo are dead, you say?" Black asked Pat.

"Yeah, I personally saw Pierre. He was cut from ear to ear," Pat explained.

"Did you see Bo-Bo, too?" Black asked.

"No, but he didn't answer when I called. I know he's gone too," Pat explained.

Black stood from his seat behind his desk and began to pace in deep thought. He realized that he had a deadly problem. Somewhere in his mafia was a bigger infiltrator than Sunni. There was only one solution to fix the damaged fidelity in his mafia.

"Pat, I want all the men who assisted you tonight wiped out, and I mean ASAP," Black ordered.

"Those are your men, Black!" Pat retorted.

"And I want them erased from the Haitian Mafia."

"It's done, Haitian," Pat said.

"I know, son. I know, son!" Black responded.

Chapter Five

Shamoney had been out on bond for two weeks now, taking every move gingerly. With Martin County's one-strike law, a person was only permitted to post bail once and be on the streets with one bond. Finally, Real had come to him with the question and requested the help he'd been waiting for since Real touched solid ground.

Real was ready to venture back into the dope game, but one problem had troubled Shamoney. Real was asking for way too much product. Knowing his brother was able to obtain whatever he needed, Shamoney was furious because Real was putting him in a tough spot. For two hours now, Shamoney had been trying to convince Real that he was moving too fast. But Real remained adamant and was ready to tell his brother his real intentions. They both were shooting pool at Shamoney's crib in Port St. Lucie that he shared with his wife, Chantele.

"Lil brah, you may not understand my plans, but trust me, if I'm asking fo' it, then I can sho' back it," Real said as he struck the seven ball into the right pocket.

"Real, I ain't sayin' you can't, brah. You been gone five years and you've only been home a month now. Asking for five keys, this shit is not the same no more, brah!" Shamoney explained.

"Yeah, I know lil brah. Everybody sellin' their souls for some chump change, nigga. Bowin' down to these sorry-ass Haitians, nigga, including yo' ass!" Real shouted, growing tired of explaining himself.

"My nigga, I ain't like none of them niggas hustling fo' pennies. I get mines!" Shamoney pounded his chest proudly as he struck but missed the nine ball in the left corner. *Shit!* he thought.

"So tell me, Sha, how long you been fuckin' with these Haitians, my nigga?" Real asked as he prepared to hit the four ball into the left pocket.

"A year after you left, why?" Shamoney asked with agitation as Real struck the ball and nailed it in the left pocket.

"So that's four years workin' fo' a muthafuckin' millionaire, and you're different from the rest of these niggas out here eatin' who are getting' pennies and dimes, huh?" Real inquired while striking the six ball.

"What are you tryin' to say, Real?" Shamoney asked as his brother missed the five ball.

"Sha, I'm not tryin' to belittle you in no kind of way. You are my brother, and I'ma be real with you. I got a plan to make both of us six figures, man. If I had a guess, I'd say fo' a fact that since you've been down with these Haitians, you ain't nowhere near six figures."

He's right, Shamoney thought, missing yet another ball in the left corner.

"Chantele is the only six figures under this roof, Sha!"

"How the fuck you know that?" Shamoney wanted to know.

"Fuck these Haitians, lil brah. Let's be about our own shit!" Real said, nailing the two ball.

"And how are we supposed to do that?" Shamoney inquired as his brother prepared to strike the three ball into the right pocket.

"We set up our own shop and run these muthafuckas off our coast. Then we shut the coast down and have every means of regulatin' the East Coast," Real said as he missed the three ball while unintentionally nailing the eight ball. "Damn!" he exclaimed.

"That's exactly what will happen, Real, if you are serious. Their entire army will still be standin' with yours while you fall alone!" Shamoney said while pointing at all his balls to Real's few.

"Shamoney, you can't let your mind stay on settling fo' less. Five years in the game with the access you have, I would be sittin' on double six figures. I may have lost this game, but I have no means of losing the game I'm about to play. I sat in prison for five long years, so I had the time to come up with a plan to hold down our city and the Treasure Coast."

"How you just gonna get out here and expect to change the game?"

"You remember state property, don't you?"

"Oh, so it's get down or lay down? Nigga, prison done fucked yo' head up!" Shamoney said, chuckling at the prospect of Real's crazy, preposterous, and insane plan.

"You're tryin' to get killed, Real! Seriously, I think you need to rethink your plans if you're serious," Shamoney said as he pulled out a Ziploc bag filled with pre-rolled dro blunts and fired one up.

"I can give you three, brah. But five is too deep, and last I checked, brah, you only have $50,000. A key go for twenty-eight down here," Shamoney offered his brother.

Real understood his brother's precaution of spotting him the other two, so he refrained from letting it upset him.

"I'll take that, lil brah. Trust me, I'ma make sure you get all yours back," Real retorted.

"I know, brah. Just be careful, because these streets have no empathy for no man," Shamoney said.

* * *

When Real pulled up to Jake's store in the swamp in which he grew up, he saw a crowd of niggas that he had grown up with shooting craps.

"How's it goin', brah?" V-Money called to Real as he approached the group.

"It's good, V-Money. Where the fuck is Lunatic?" Real asked.

V-Money quickly grabbed Real by his shoulders and pulled him out of earshot of the group, to the side of the store where drug sales were handled.

"Man, you ain't heard from me, but he's laying low in Palm Beach after runnin' into that bank two weeks ago."

"Damn, brah! Turned up like that?" Real inquired.

"Man, Lunatic gets his by all means. It's hard out here, Real. We juggling nickels to stay alive, brah!" V-Money said.

Real had been home a month and knew that every nigga was struggling in the dope game because of the Haitians having shit on lock.

No nigga can see no money when they're being fed crumbs and can't expand their reach, he thought.

"V-Money, how fast can you move a brick?" Real asked.

"Shit, fast as it hits my hands, but not 'round here. This shit locked on one muthafucka!"

"Who dat?" Real inquired.

"Them Haitians," V-Money answered.

"Well, let's run 'em out of here," Real recommended.

"Man, these muthafuckas ain't going nowhere."

"Who said we give them a chance, V-Money?" Real asked.

"So that's why you looking for Lunatic?"

"Nah, I'm looking for all my niggas to get the picture," Real said sincerely.

V-Money was an old-school, oil-toned nigga in his early forties. He stood six foot tall, weighed 175 pounds, and had a mouth full of gold teeth, and dreadlocks. The dope game was all he knew, and he had seen it go from good to bad and from bad to worse. He was down with Real, and he knew that Real was serious about running the Haitians' traps out of their hood. He just wished that he had a lot of niggas with Real's heart, or else it would be a death mission or, better said, suicide mission.

"Real, listen, brah. I feel you, but from an old G, lil brah, take shit slow. Ya brother plugged in with them Haitians, brah. I'm sure of that."

"V-Money, I ain't waiting on no Haitian to drop shit in my hand. That's where everyone got the game fucked up. In a couple weeks, I'ma try you out with a couple keys, nigga, and show you how we supposed to have this shit, V-Money," Real said as he walked away and entered Jake's store to have a chat with this mentor, Jake himself.

* * *

Boom! Boom! Boom!

Lunatic put three slugs into the Jamaican scalp of the guy he had just caught slipping while sitting in his conspicuous Chevy Impala on twenty-eight-inch rims.

"Let me get this pussy-ass nigga!" Lunatic demanded as he yanked the phat Cuban link chain and Jesus piece embellished with diamonds from around the Jamaican's neck.

Lunatic opened the door with gloved hands and then searched the dead man's pockets and retrieved a phat wad of cash. When he saw the Jamaican walk to the car by himself at Club Pawn Shop to snort a couple of lines of cocaine, Lunatic crept up on him and lit up his day, turning it red. He was having a field day in Palm Beach County robbing dope boys on every corner by himself every night.

When Lunatic stripped the Jamaican of all his spoils, he turned on his heels at a hastened pace, jumped inside his gray Dodge Durango, and successfully fled the scene.

Chapter Six

"You love this pussy!" Bellda purred out to Pat as she looked him in his eyes while slowly riding his dick.

Smack!

"Damn right I do!" Pat said after slapping her succulent ass cheeks.

"Be nice and I might let you hang around longer than you intended," Bellda told him.

She was a ravishing twenty-six-year-old Haitian-American with brown skin, who stood five five and weighed 145 pounds in her stallion thighs and enormous ass. She literally had Buffy the Body beat. She had Pat breaking all the rules of his marriage to his beautiful wife, Gina, by playing his three-year mistress. Unbeknownst to Pat, Bellda was tired of playing the young mistress in his life.

The dick was good and the money he showered her with was too, but she seriously felt that she was robbing herself of real contentedness and felt more deserving than a mistress. And there were times when it wouldn't be him or the money, she was just tired.

There are plenty of good men out here who want a real bitch, Bellda thought as she felt herself coming to her orgasm.

"Shit!" she moaned out as she began speeding up her pace while simultaneously working her pussy muscles to bring Pat to his on cue with hers.

"Damn, baby! This pussy is too damn good!" Pat moaned out while gripping Bellda's waist as she slammed down on his love tool.

"Uhh! Uhh! Pat, I'm coming!"

"Baby, come all over this dick!" Pat shouted, biting down on his bottom lip.

"Uhh! Uhh! Shit!" Bellda let out, shaking violently as if she was catching a seizure.

"Arrghh!" Pat grunted as he came to his load, releasing inside his Trojan condom.

"Damn, baby! You do that shit all the time, making me come like that!" Pat exclaimed, speaking of Bellda's pussy techniques that always blew his mind.

"I know you appreciate it, right?"

"Of course, baby," Pat said as he pulled Bellda down and then flipped her onto her back while simultaneously kissing her sexy lips.

Pat raised up, took off the used condom, and slung it onto the hotel floor for room service to clean up.

"Bellda, you are winning me over."

"You always saying that Pat," she said.

"And I'm always meaning it too."

"Then when will this stop?" she asked, gesturing with her hands and speaking of their furtiveness and creeping around with each other in a hotel every week. She was tired.

"Bellda, I told you to give me some time, baby! That's all I ask."

"Pat, I've been giving you three years thus far, and it seems like the more time passes, the more you two seem happy." Bellda paused when her voice began to crack.

Damn! I hate seeing her like this, Pat thought.

"Pat, I'm tired, and I want to be loved like my worth as a woman," she said as a tear escaped her right eye.

"I know, baby. I'ma make this happen. Just give me time, boo. Please!" Pat said.

Bellda thought for a moment. It sounded sincere, and she wanted it to be. Giving the low tolerance of her waiting on him, Pat was the man who had been taking care of her the last three years. His feelings were not in question. Bellda wrapped her arms around his neck and looked him in the eyes.

"I love you, Pat, and the least I can do is trust you, but just know that it's time to really make a decision. If you're gonna stay with your wife, I respect that. But I will move on, Pat, because this is not what I signed up for," Bellda explained.

"Don't worry, baby. I know where my heart's at," Pat sighed. *But I can't leave my wife,* he thought.

"Let's hope so," Bellda retorted.

* * *

When T-Gutta stepped out of Wendy's with a soda in one hand and a bag of food in the other, he caught a glimpse of the two niggas in the dark blue Ford Taurus. He knew trouble when he saw it, and the big chunk around his neck did nothing but attract it to him. When T-Gutta made it to his Nissan Altima rental, he heard the Taurus engine come to life.

Come on, niggas, and watch me paint that shit! T-Gutta thought as he got into his rental car while pulling his Glock .19 from his waistband and setting it on his lap.

T-Gutta started the car and then pulled out of the parking space. As expected, the Ford Taurus hopped right behind him in traffic. T-Gutta was lying low in Ft. Pierce-St. Lucie County until the heat died down from the bank robbery that he and Lunatic impertinently hit by themselves. Both compadres made away with only $20,000, sad to say, and they could not spend any of it because of the dye packing exploding on all of it. T-Gutta and Lunatic both cut their dreadlocks to prevent being noticed. The bank they hit was a local bank in Martin County, resulting in an officer being shot and killed.

T-Gutta turned off on US 1 and traveled on the main strip called Avenue D into Fort Pierce. When he came to the light at Avenue D and 7th Street, T-Gutta grabbed his twin Glocks from under his seat, racked them, and then looked in his rearview mirror.

Now or never! T-Gutta encouraged himself.

When he saw the two niggas engrossed with him, he quickly opened the door. With agility, he leaped from his rental and rapidly squeezed both triggers of his Glocks.

Boom! Boom! Boom! Boom!

The hollow-point slugs easily went through the windshield, catching the passenger in his face and the driver in his chest. The driver then slammed the car into reverse but was unable to defeat the storm of bullets. The Taurus backed into the car behind them, allowing T-Gutta to have a field day. He jumped on top of the hood and shot down through the windshield, hitting both of his targets at close-point range.

Boom! Boom! Boom! Boom!

"What! Y'all niggas thought y'all had a duck?" T-Gutta screamed, giving both compadres the entire clip in broad daylight.

When T-Gutta hopped off the hood, he saw plenty of eyewitnesses, but he wasn't worried. It was the city of murder, where it went down anywhere and anytime. No one said anything, and no one wanted to be involved with a murder. The police were nonchalant in responding to gunshot calls because they knew that nine out of ten times, the victims could not be saved. T-Gutta took his time leaving the chilling scene behind and proceeded to his low-key spot he had on 29th Street in the heart of the projects, where they treated him like he was home.

* * *

Sitting alone at his table in his newly furnished apartment in Hillmoore Village on the east side of Port St. Lucie, Real was in deep contemplative thought. Jake had given him the locations of the four Haitian traps in the swamp where Real was to begin his plan and move on it according to how he had seen it years ago, in his cell with his friend Kentucky. On a cryptic sheet of paper that was transparent only to him, Real had laid out his entire plan for taking over the tri-county area.

Real had spoken with Kentucky moments ago, about the plan they both had put together drudgingly. Kentucky had a smuggled cell phone that Real had paid a CO to bring to him, as well as a pound of dro. Kentucky gave Real plenty of useful advice that Real intended to use, by all means.

When Real heard the knocks at his door, he gathered his blueprints. Folding them neatly, he stored them back into the large Hebrew Bible that he owned and kept on top of the refrigerator. The plush apartment was a two-bedroom, two-bath upstairs palace. When he strutted over to the door and opened it, he was greeted by a gorgeous Lala, who looked like the diva of all divas in the world in her Prada minidress, stockings, and some lustrous Jason Wu five-inch stilettos.

"What! You thought I wasn't coming, nigga?" Lala said as she fell into Real's arms and passionately kissed him.

Real grabbed her succulent ass in his palms and instantly became erect. He let go of her and went to close the door and lock it. He had been seeing Lala furtively for about two weeks. In his heart, despite her still being involved with her baby daddy, Joc, she was still his bitch in many aspects. It was transparent to both of them that they would never be over each other.

"Come here, baby!" Real demanded Lala, who immed-iately walked over at his behest.

"Yes, daddy!" she answered while unfastening Real's belt to his fitted jeans.

When his jeans fell to his ankles, Lala stroked his throbbing dick and then descended to her knees, taking him in her mouth and gagging slightly from deep-throating his large-sized manhood. As she sucked his dick, they stared into each other's eyes, enjoying the common desire they both shared since the beginning of their relationship years ago.

Before he allowed her to bring him to his peak, Real pulled back and looked down at Lala. "Stand up, ma!" he demanded.

When she stood up, Real spun her around and bent her at her waist while simultaneously lifting her minidress to her mid-stomach, exposing her caramel, succulent, enormous ass. In one thrust, Real deeply entered Lala's soaking wet pussy.

"Aww shit!" Lala purred, gasping and trying to find new air to breathe.

She was thankful that Real sat in her for a moment before he began vigorously penetrating her.

"Real! Real!" Lala loudly shouted, lost in her own paradise. "Dis yo' pussy, Real? Dis yo' pussy?" Lala shouted in a loud moan, despite Real setting their stipulations.

He wanted no relationship, because when they were there once upon a time ago, things didn't work out for them. The moment he went to prison, she moved on to the next man and ended up pregnant. To Real, there was no way that he'd allow himself to get back into a committed relationship with Lala.

It is just not going to happen, Lala, Real thought as he continued to beat out her back while engulfed in their past relationship. *Why did you have to run off and get pregnant, Lala?* Real thought as he vengefully pounded her pussy, like he did every time he fucked her and thought about her leaving him for dead.

Bitches gon' be bitches, no matter what! Real thought, knowing that he couldn't allow the power of pussy to distract him from obtaining the throne of the tri-county area, from Martin, St. Lucie, Palm Beach, and Indian River to Okeechobee Counties.

He planned vigorously to take them from Pat, who Jake had put him up on, and the main nigga himself, Haitian Black.

Both of those niggas just don't know what's about to wake them up, Real thought as he pounded Lala to her knees.

"Real, baby. Oh shit!" Lala loudly purred as she came to an orgasm and Real exploded and shot his load all over her ass.

"Uhh shit!" Real exhaled, stroking his load on an exhausted Lala.

"Damn, dis pussy still snatchin', boo!" Real said.

"And it's always waitin' fo' you to beat it up too, nigga! Now, I'm hungry. Let's shower so I can cook," Lala said, ready to cater to Real.

Real stepped out of his jeans.

"That's cool. Come on!" Real said as he snatched Lala from the floor and carried her upstairs.

He fucked her in his master bedroom before they showered, where they did it once again inside the steamy tub.

Chapter Seven

When Shamoney pulled up to the luxurious mansion in Lakeworth in Palm Beach, he was intrigued as he stared at the all-white Maybach that belonged to Pat as he rolled out of his own .745.

"Damn! This nigga done went and got him a muthafuckin' Maybach. I gotta step my shit up fo' real," Shamoney said as he reached into the backseat and came back out with two full duffel bags full of money that belonged to the Haitian mafia.

When he strutted toward the front door of the mansion, it opened, and a gorgeous pregnant Gina appeared in a colorful sundress.

"Hey, he's in the back. He told me to take both bags and for you to go see him by the pool," Gina retorted.

"Okay. Umm, here!" Shamoney said, handing the bags over to Gina. "You sho' you got them?"

"Boy, money will never be something that I can't handle," Gina said as she looked over her shoulders. "And you know that!"

"Is that so?" Shamoney retorted as he walked through the house to the back pool area, where he found Pat and Big Chub lounging in beach chairs smoking individual dro blunts.

"What's up, Shamoney?" Pat said, coughing from the pressure he was inhaling into his lungs.

"Same as usual, Pat. Tryin' to get it. I see you done got yourself a Maybach, nigga!"

"Yeah, do you like it, brah?" Pat asked as he passed the blunt to Shamoney, who instantly inhaled deeply. "Hell yeah!"

"Good! I knew you would!" Pat said as he tossed a set of keys to Shamoney, who snatched them out of the air.

"What are these for?" Shamoney asked, perplexed.

"It's a gift, Shamoney, for working diligently for da Haitian mafia. Consider it a promotion. You know, like a gift," Pat exclaimed.

Shamoney was speechless as he listened to Pat, a man who had just handed him the keys to an expensive Maybach—and a man who his brother was threatening to destroy.

I gotta talk to Real. Pat is good people, despite fucking his wife once behind his back. Shit, da bitch came on to me! Shamoney thought unregretfully.

"It's okay, Shamoney. Shit! I wouldn't know what to say either, feel me?" Big Chub said.

"Pat, thank you, man. Damn! I can't believe this shit. But damn, do you think the feds will get skeptical and pick me up?"

"Money, you have to be smarter than that. The Maybach is not something fo' you to drive around in like you do with that .745. You pull up to the club in dat bitch with a bad bitch. That's how you do it, Shamoney!" Pat explained, grabbing the blunt from him.

"I feel dat, brah! How am I supposed to get my .745 back?"

"It's already on its way back."

"Damn, nigga! You move quick," Shamoney exclaimed, impressed but not the least surprised.

"So, Shamoney, are you enjoying the flow of money in Martin?" Pat asked him.

"The money good, and shop's never closed," Shamoney retorted.

"Good, Shamoney."

"Look, normally I would spot you five bricks, but today I'ma spot you one."

"One?" Shamoney exclaimed. "One brick and I make $10,000 for flipping it? How 'bout we go up if anything? Pat, I'm saying that I could carry more loads, brah. I got to make something, feel me?"

Pat understood everything and hated what he was about to tell Shamoney next.

"Listen, Shamoney. It's either take the brick or leave with nothing."

What the fuck this clown nigga on? Shamoney thought.

"You know the rules, Money. You were arrested and posted $200,000 to walk the streets again. We don't—"

"Wait a minute. Like hold on, nigga!" Shamoney said, shaking his head from side to side. "You think I'm a snitch, huh?"

"No, I never concluded that, but at the same time, it's not pushed through the back of my head," Pat said sincerely.

I can't believe dis shit! This muthafucka is letting me go after all the good I've done for him and Black, Shamoney thought.

"Man, keep the brick and the Maybach! I'll get what I want real soon," Shamoney exclaimed as an understatement, forgetting to toss back the Maybach keys to Pat.

"Shamoney, when dis shit cools off, trust me, we will bring you back, brah!"

"I don't need shit from the mafia. If they can't trust me now, why trust me later?" Shamoney said as he turned on his heels to leave.

Inside the mansion, he saw Gina again. She could tell that he was upset by the way he left without saying goodbye.

These muthafuckas don't know shit yet. I've been loyal and good to them all. Now a nigga catch a case and it's a problem, he thought.

Shamoney wasn't too naive not to see it from another perspective. If he was a boss nigga such as Pat, then he could understand precaution. *But I was da best he'd ever had!* Shamoney reflected.

Shamoney accelerated in the Maybach, after realizing his own .745 was gone, so he had no choice other than to drive his new car home.

"So what do you think?" Pat asked Chub.

"I think you did what da fuck you had to do. We must all know how to deal and move with precaution. The nigga has no room to be mad at you," Big Chub explained to an attentive Pat.

"Yeah, I agree. I did da right thing!" Pat retorted, but he still felt like he had done the wrong thing.

* * *

Shamoney was furious after soaking in the reality of Pat basically cutting him off. He sat in his plush, luxurious living room with Real, who he had just informed of what occurred hours ago. Despite being connected with the Haitian mafia and feeling like the man of the hour and city, Shamoney now clearly saw through his brother's plan to take over. At first he perceived it as insane, but now, left out in the world alone, he was depending on a way to stay stable. He only saw one avenue to take, and that was with his brother. Shamoney had laced Real up on everything about the mafia that Real had already known, except Shamoney being furtively involved with Pat's wife.

"So, this nigga, Pat, keeps a mean entourage around him?" Real asked while passing Shamoney a phat-ass dro blunt twisted in an Altimo cigar leaf.

"Yeah, but them niggas ain't no pressure to me, brah. I know where to go to get the niggas one by one in their muthafuckin' sleep," Shamoney exclaimed while exhaling a thick cloud of smoke.

"Brah, like I told you a couple days ago, I got ya all the way. I still have them three bricks that you gave me. We could power up off that."

"I can't believe this shit. A nigga connected one day, eatin' good, and then the next day a nigga vulnerable because a nigga don't trust a real nigga," Shamoney vented, "but they'll trust a pussy nigga first."

"Lil brah, don't even sweat that shit. We will make these ho niggas respect us Martin County niggas, by all means. All we need is a couple young 'bout-it niggas who ain't scared to slang dat choppa on these muthafuckas."

"And a connect!" Shamoney retorted, cutting off Real.

"We good, lil brah. I got niggas I know fuckin' with that Columbian snow white, nigga," Real said truthfully.

"Damn, nigga! So you really serious 'bout dis shit, huh?"

"Lil brah, whenever you know me to be about talk?" Real asked, deeply inhaling the dro blunt. "This is our muthafuckin' city. We just got to show a bitch better than we could tell them, lil brah!" he said as he exhaled the cloud of smoke and walked over to Shamoney's minibar to pour his brother and himself a Hennessy. "Money, we gotta take da meat out of the lion's mouth and do it boldly." He walked back into the living room and handed Shamoney his drink.

"The underdog gets tired of being a pawn. Dat's why when a pawn get pushed into enemy territory, the pawn elevates into a power piece. It comes out whatever it wants to be," Real explained to Shamoney the fundamentals of the game of chess, comparing it to life's obstacles. "It happens in real life, lil brah—everything dat happens on a chess board."

Damn! Brah just hit me with some real shit. I gotta stand up and get that nigga Pat outta my way, Shamoney thought. "So, when you ready to get this shit poppin' I got $300,000, and Chantele won't be back until next season or else I'd have her put the money up for us, brah," Shamoney said.

"No!" Real said, shaking his head. "Leave your wife's funds alone. We gonna get our shit by taking their shit—all their spoils," Real said. "Call Johnny and tell lil brah we on our way and to have everything in place when we get there."

"What? Is Johnny down? He already know the beat?" Shamoney asked.

"Of course, he do. Sad to say, you were da only one reluctant. But lil brah is ready to spill blood. Welcome aboard the Swamp Mafia, soldier," Real said, bumping glasses with Shamoney as they then downed their drinks.

"Hell yeah, brah!" Shamoney said, feeling the burning liquor travel throughout his body.

Swamp Mafia, he thought.

Chapter Eight

Popa Zoe was an old-school Haitian who was holding down one of the biggest trap houses in the swamp. This was the trap house where all the preparations were done, and Popa Zoe, the lieutenant, controlled the flow of the product. It was his call to shut down the four traps in the swamp, which he had done precisely an hour ago. The trap was on 10th Street and Palm Beach Road, next to some Mexicans who minded their own business and never once complained about the consistent traffic that came throughout the day.

Inside with Popa Zoe, on his way out the door, was his nephew, Fat Zoe.

Fat Zoe was one of his top go-getters, who had brought his Miami mentality with him to the swamp.

"Well, neph, I'll see you in the morning," Popa Zoe said as he stood from the worn sofa.

Popa Zoe was barefooted and bare-chested with a muscular frame. He had lengthy dreadlocks and a dark brown complexion. When he smiled, he revealed an ominously sparkling gold grill at the top and bottom of his mouth.

"Unc, so when is Pat supposed to come and get the rest of the money?" Fat Zoe asked while scratching his huge belly.

He then tucked his .357 into the waistband under his protruding gut.

"I reckon' tomorrow sometime, neph?" Popa Zoe retorted while walking to the front door to let Fat Zoe out.

When Popa Zoe unlocked the door, his money phone rang. Not being one to miss out on a sell, he rushed over to the living room glass table and retrieved his flip cell phone while Fat Zoe let himself out.

"Hello?" Popa Zoe spoke to a silent line. "Hello," he spoke again, the moment Fat Zoe opened the door.

Popa Zoe saw Fat Zoe dramatically pull back, and then heard the explosion. Subsequently, Fat Zoe's head exploded in a spray of blood and brain matter onto the surrounding walls.

"What the fuck!" Popa Zoe shouted as he made a hasty attempt to grab his AK-47 rifle from the corner of the living room. But he was taken down when two slugs entered the back of his thigh. "Arrggh! Shit!" Popa Zoe cried in pain.

When Popa Zoe looked back, he saw three masked men enter the house and then close the door. One of the masked men held a Glock .40 in his hand. He walked up on Popa Zoe and planted his boot in his back.

"I'ma ask you one time, Popa Zoe. Where the fuck is the money and all the work at, nigga? I know you got it," Real ordered the man as Lunatic and T-Gutta proceeded to rummage through the trap house.

Popa Zoe knew that he had no win. He almost had decided to let the nigga work for the come-up, but the chances of survival probably were still subject for him. So as not to entice the nigga, he gave it up easily. "Inside the bedroom in the closet. Lift up the rug and the far-left floor board. It's all the work."

"Where's the money at?" Real yelled.

"In the deep freezer in the utility closet. That's it," Popa Zoe stuttered.

"You sure?" Real asked.

"Yeah, I'm—" Popa Zoe began.

Boom! Boom! Boom!

Before Popa Zoe could finish, Real put three slugs into the back of his head and immediately joined Lunatic and T-Gutta.

Just like Popa Zoe said, everything was right where he directed them. The trio safely made away with $300,000 in cash and fourteen bricks of cocaine.

* * *

Precisely the same time that Real, Lunatic, and T-Gutta hit the trap on 10th and Palm Beach, Shamoney, Johnny, and V-Money kicked in another trap on 4th and Palm Beach, killing five Zoes and making away with $175,000 and ten bricks of cocaine.

At around three in the morning, the only thing moving in the swamp were fiends and the six men in masks who had just hit the two main traps that the Haitians held down there. Now, an hour later, everyone was at Shamoney's palace in Port St. Lucie dividing up the spoils among the six of them.

"Shit! Gonna be hot in the swamp, V-Money. So, try to avoid being seen by anyone."

"What 'bout the other three traps? Shit! We got to get them out this bitch, too!" V-Money retorted.

"We will, but they're less important. They're feeble without the head. Like taking the head off a snake," Real said.

"You got that right, lil nigga!" V-Money exclaimed.

"Here, V-Money. This is all yours. Welcome to the Swamp Mafia as our lieutenant in the swamp," Shamoney said, handing him a duffel bag containing a few kilos and $75,000 in cash.

"Don't get stupid, V-Money, or gamble ya shit away!" Lunatic warned.

"My nigga, I got this shit!" V-Money said.

Shamoney gave the rest of the crew their well-earned cut, and then he put his up in his safe upstairs. For the rest of the wee hours, the crew smoked kush blunts, drank liquor, and gambled on the pool table. Being a superb player, Real racked up all bets and took them all in without crapping out with the eight ball. When dawn came, everyone went their separate ways until it was time to come together again.

Moving meticulously is a part of the plan, and it will pay off for the best when it is all said and done, Real thought while meditating on Shamoney's sofa alone in the living room.

* * *

"You see this shit!" Pat screamed into the phone while looking at the crime scene in Indiantown.

It was breaking news from the moment his foot soldiers discovered his dead men—his good men.

"Damn it, Pat! Who would hit us like this?" Big Chub asked, perplexed about the entire situation.

Pat looked at the sixty-four-inch flat-screen television in his living room and let out a long sigh. "Big Chub, I don't know, but I will find out real soon. I need you to do something for me, Chub."

"What is it, brah?" Big Chub answered, wanting to know what was on his partner's mind.

"We'll talk when you get here. Get over here now!" Pat demanded as he hung up the phone.

* * *

Real and Lala lay in bed together while looking at the chilling scene in the swamp on the news. Lala had no clue that the man she was cuddling up with was the same man responsible for the crimes committed in her hood earlier in the day.

"Someone done finally grew the courage to rob them Haitians," Lala said as she watched the two scenes flash back and forth.

Yeah, it took a real nigga to come home! Real thought. "Shit 'bout to get real! You just be careful," Real told Lala.

Lala climbed on top of Real and then looked him in his eyes and said, "I'm that bitch of the Ms. Gorgeouses who I wish a nigga would step wrong. Haitian or not, my 9 mm talk real loud," Lala said to Real as she grabbed his semi-erect dick and guided into her wet pussy.

"I believe you, ma. But still be careful!" Real reiterated as he deeply slammed into her.

"Uhh!" she purred, feeling him so deeply in her womb. "I will, baby. I will!" Lala purred as she increased the pace of riding Real's dick.

Damn! I love this nigga, Lala thought, with regrets of fucking him over while in prison, which was eating her alive.

When the tears cascaded from her eyes, Real saw them and mistook them for passion.

* * *

"Kentucky, do you have more K2?" an inmate named Jason asked, inquiring about the synthetic marijuana that had every inmate in the prison compound going crazy.

"Yeah, Jason. What do you need?" Kentucky asked the man, who stood at the cell door.

Kentucky was busy writing his new novel titled *Last Drop,* so he never saw the impish look on Jason's face.

"Man, I'm trying to get an ounce," Jason retorted, getting Kentucky's undivided attention.

"Cracka, since when you had it to get an ounce, Jason?" Kentucky asked.

"What! You think a country backwoods Georgia boy can't cop shit? I just look like this," Jason responded.

"You do know that I sell an ounce."

"For $400, I know. I just got to reach out, that's all," Jason said.

"How long you gonna be?"

"Twenty minutes. That's all I need."

"Okay, come in and pull back the door," Kentucky said as he reached underneath his pillow and grabbed his Verizon flip cell phone.

When Kentucky turned around, he saw that Jason had a twelve-inch shank in his hand. Kentucky saw that it was an ice pick, one of the deadliest shanks in prison since it left no gruesome scene and only internal bleeding. Jason stood like a truck. He was six four and weighed 250 solid pounds. Kentucky was no equal to him if a brawl popped off.

"Let's make this real easy, boy. You gonna give me that phone and all the dope in this bitch!" Jason ordered while keeping a safe distance from Kentucky.

Jason knew well of how Kentucky got down, and if any man underestimated him, it wouldn't be Jason. Kentucky and Jason both had a common release date, so Jason's boldness was not surprising to Kentucky at all.

"Man, you tripping, Jason. You know I'll work with—"

"Man, shut the fuck up, boy, and do as I say. I don't care 'bout all that shit-talking, Kentucky," Jason spat, growing angry and impatient.

"Man, you got that," Kentucky said as he grabbed his phone and tossed it over to Jason, who caught it with his free hand.

"There are six ounces in this pillow," Kentucky informed Jason while pointing at it. "The rest is in my hold-down man's room."

"How many in your hold-down room?" Jason asked, shoving the cell phone into his back pocket.

"Ten," Kentucky retorted.

Damn it! Jason thought angrily, after realizing he was better off hitting Kentucky's hold-down man.

But little did he know that Kentucky trusted no one, and he lived by the DTA code: don't trust anybody.

The man who had put Jason up to robbing Kentucky had told him beyond any doubt that Kentucky kept more of his product on him in the cell.

Fuck it! I'm all in now! Jason thought.

"Okay, give me them six," Jason demanded.

"Sure," Kentucky said, grabbing the pillow while grabbing hold of his fourteen-inch shank. When Kentucky tossed the pillow toward Jason's face, he charged at him with the shank and rammed it into his lower stomach.

"Arrghhh!" Jason growled in pain, dropping his shank.

He tried to scramble backward out of the cell, but the door was partially closed. Before he knew it, Kentucky had hit him high above his rib cage.

"Nooo! Stop!" Jason begged.

The inmates in the dayroom furtively made their way to Kentucky's cell. By the time a few made it to the top tier, Kentucky already had stabbed Jason thirty-two times, adding him to his list of bodies. The arrowhead fourteen-inch shank had saved Kentucky from going to the same lifeless state that Jason was now in.

"Kentucky, you straight, brah?" his cellmate, Richard, asked as he stepped over Jason's bloody body.

It was evident from Jason's wide-open eyes that he was dead.

"Hell nah! This bitch just tried to rob me. Who the fuck was his lookout?" Kentucky asked while washing his hands inside the chrome toilet to remove Jason's blood off of him and the shank.

"I don't know, but we gotta get him out of here and get this place cleaned up," Richard suggested.

"No, we gotta get out of here, and go to the rec yard as soon as they call it. The only thing they'll do is throw us in lockdown, brah."

"Man, I can't do no lockdown, brah. Hell nah!" Richard exclaimed, shaking his head from side to side.

Damn it! I knew he was a pussy-ass white boy. This the shit that makes a cracka look like trash! Kentucky thought.

"Okay, well give me a minute. Come in and close the door," Kentucky told Richard.

Richard looked around the dorm and saw more inmates hanging out on the top tier like nosey birds on a power line.

Damn! I just hope nobody puts me behind this shit, Richard thought as he pulled back the door.

When Richard turned around, Kentucky rammed his shank into his larynx, where it came out the back of his neck, spraying blood onto the cell's window.

Richard fell to his knees while holding onto his neck. When Kentucky pulled out the shank from Richard's neck, Richard collapsed on top of Jason's body. He was dead before he hit the deck. Kentucky washed the shank thoroughly and then stuffed all his products into his mattress after retrieving his cell phone from Jason's back pocket.

"Recreation! All inmates report to the rec yard, if you're not a house man," the female CO announced over the PA system.

Kentucky took the other shank and stuffed it in his long Bob Barker's sock. He stepped over his cellmate's and Jason's bodies and walked out to the recreation yard in the crowd of inmates.

The inmates in D-dorm zone knew exactly what was coming next as soon as the COs discovered the gruesome scene in Kentucky's cell.

Once on the rec yard, Kentucky found a prison bum named Ol' Charlie looking for cigarette butts on the ground.

"Yo, Ol' Charlie, can you do me a favor, and I'll buy you whatever you want off canteen as long as it's not the world," Kentucky said to the old white man.

"What is it, 'Tucky?" he asked.

Kentucky squatted with the old man and then retrieved the shank from his sock and handed it over.

"I need this put in the ground," Kentucky said.

"I got ya, 'Tucky," the man responded.

It wasn't the first time that Ol' Charlie had put a dirty knife in the ground for Kentucky, and it wouldn't be the last.

Kentucky had met up with Chucky and told him what had happened in his cell as they both walked the prison track. It was no later than an hour when the recreation yard was shut down and the prison went on emergency lockdown.

"All inmates report to your assigned areas and report back to your dorms," the captain exclaimed over the PA system.

More than a dozen COs rushed the recreation yard in search of one inmate: Kentucky.

Chapter Nine

When Shamoney awoke at noon espying the twelve missed calls from Pat, he briefly chuckled.

What the fuck this nigga want? Shamoney thought as he emerged from bed with his iPhone and walked naked to the bathroom from his and Chantele's room.

Lying in his bed was one of this sideline bitches, far from his mistress, Gina. Her name was Tasha, an extremely swarthy complected hood bitch, who had a sexy-ass curvaceous body. She was a bad bitch, but not bad enough for Shamoney to leave his wife or his mistress, Gina.

As he relieved himself at the toilet, Shamoney called Pat to see what was on his mind. The phone rang twice before he heard Pat pick it up abruptly. "Hello?"

"You know who this is, nigga. What the fuck do you want?" Shamoney asked spitefully.

"Damn, my nigga! Tell me what's going on in the swamp? Why the fuck I got five dead men, and they all my top-dollar traps!"

"Hold on, nigga. You mean to tell me that you callin' me askin' me about shit I can't answer fo' you. Last I checked, you muthafuckas cut me off. Nigga, if I did know something, I wouldn't tell y'all niggas shit!" Shamoney sternly retorted.

"Man, who the fuck you think you're talking to, nigga? You must of fo'got who the Haitian Mafia is, nigga?" Pat shouted at Shamoney, who began laughing, which caused Pat to become even more enraged.

"Listen, Pat. I bleed just like you," Shamoney said, shaking off his dick and then flushing the toilet. "You must fo'got how you met this nigga!" Shamoney concisely retorted before he disconnected the phone.

* * *

"This bitch-ass nigga just hung up on me, Chub!" Pat exclaimed angrily. "Take me to B-Zoe, Chub. I got something fo' this nigga!" Pat promised while sitting in the passenger side of Big Chub's S-class lime-green Mercedes.

"Do you think he had something to do with hitting Popa Zoe then?" Big Chub asked Pat, who was now rubbing his temples out of frustration.

"I don't know, and I pray that he don't!" Pat retorted in Creole.

The remainder of the ride from Palm Beach County to St. Lucie County was in silence. All Pat could think about was finding the nigga responsible for his dead men. He thought about what Shamoney had reminded him of.

"You must fo'got how you met this nigga!" the words of Shamoney replayed in Pat's head.

Pat could never forget the nigga who saved his wife, Gina's, life one night from his enemies who had tried to kidnap her at a club in downtown Palm Beach. Shamoney was in the parking lot and nailed the two abductors with his MAC-10 and then rescued her, albeit Shamoney had constant eye contact with her before the hit popped off.

I was ambushed in the club's brawl and could do nothing to save Gina. But Shamoney, a complete stranger, did, Pat thought retrospectively of when he had met a much younger Shamoney.

"Something tells me that Shamoney isn't involved," Pat told Big Chub as they pulled into B-Zoe's driveway in Killa County. He lived on the south side in a middle-class neighborhood away from the ruthless gutter.

"So let's put him back on and send him after—"

"We can't. Black will never approve of it," Pat said, cutting off Big Chub.

"Well, I don't know what to say," Chub said honestly.

"Me either," Pat retorted.

They both stepped out of the Mercedes and walked up to B-Zoe's front door. Before Pat could rap on the door, B-Zoe opened it and allowed them in.

"Damn, strangers!" B-Zoe exclaimed while clapping hands with his superiors, already knowing that they would soon come for him after he saw Popa Zoe's death on the news.

"Yeah, we strangers, but we'll always be family," Pat said to B-Zoe, who closed the door and locked it behind them.

Pat saw that B-Zoe had his strap tucked in the center of his back.

This nigga always ready, Pat thought.

B-Zoe was an extremely dark-toned Haitian who stood five eight and weighed a solid 210 pounds. He kept a low-boy fade and rocked an eighteen-plate gold grill. He was the mafia's most ruthless assassin, other than Pat, who had a lot of his men beat. His name was definitely feared in the streets of Fort Pierce City among the other killers. Unlike Martin County and other counties along the Treasure Coast, Fort Pierce was born with straight killers, where they killed other killers daily. Not everyone could fit into the environment in Killa County like B-Zoe, who had migrated from Haiti to Miami to St. Lucie County. That's what made him unique at thirty years old—as well as extremely lethal.

"So, what's good, y'all niggas? Want something to drink?" B-Zoe asked Pat and Big Chub, who had sat down on his sofa.

His entire living room was white and very immaculate.

"Yeah, brah. Grab me a glass of Remy, straight."

"Me too," Pat agreed.

"Shit, me too!" B-Zoe said as he strutted over to his kitchen and poured his superiors Remy on the rocks.

B-Zoe returned in three minutes, handed them their drinks, and then took a seat in his comfortable all-white La-Z-Boy.

"So, what's good, Haitians?" B-Zoe asked in Creole, anticipating a Creole dialogue.

"Did you hear 'bout Popa Zoe?" Pat asked.

"It's all over the news, fam. What's up with that shit?" B-Zoe retorted as he took a sip of his Remy.

"I dunno! We tryin' to figure that out ourselves," Pat answered.

"What do you think?" Big Chub asked, taking a sip of his drink.

"I think somebody in the swamp knows more than anyone. I'll even go as far as to say one of them did it," B-Zoe insinuated.

"Ain't that Shamoney's area?" B-Zoe questioned.

"He's no longer with us. Black cut him loose."

"Fo' what?" B-Zoe asked Pat, cutting him off.

"He caught a case. You know how Black is if you not 100 percent Haitian!" Pat exclaimed.

"Damn! Did y'all cut him before Popa Zoe's death?" B-Zoe asked.

"Yeah," Pat retorted.

"Then there you go! That nigga is the one we need to be talkin' to," B-Zoe suggested.

"We know, but before we see him, I need you to handle something fo' me, B-Zoe," Pat said. He then downed his glass of Remy.

"What's on the table, Haitian?" B-Zoe asked.

"$100,000, B-Zoe. You in or what?"

"Is there blood involved?" B-Zoe asked, with a smirk on his face.

"Most definitely," Pat responded, breaking out with an evil smile.

"Then hell yeah! I'm in fo' a bloodbath!" B-Zoe said.

He was addicted to murder, even it if was just for the hell of it.

"Well listen," Pat broke off B-Zoe with what he needed done ASAP.

* * *

Bellda was the fourth customer in line at the Sketchers store inside the Treasure Coast Mall in Martin County. It was a mall where everyone on the coast enjoyed shopping and sometimes just hanging out.

I wish these muthafuckas would stop bumpin' their damn gums and move on, because a bitch is tired! Bellda thought impatiently, after working a twelve-hour day.

She was only making a quick stop in Sketchers to purchase a new pair of work footwear for her new job at a nursing home in Stuart, the capital city of Martin County. She had so many things running through her vagrant mind about her relationship with Pat.

Last night she had cried herself to sleep, yearning for a man who she couldn't have for herself. Thinking of how it would be with Pat if she was no longer the mistress brought tears to her eyes. Absentmindedly, she lost her emotions and was unable to stop the rapid flood of tears cascading down her face.

"Ma'am, are you okay?" an older woman working at the store asked, after seeing Bellda silently crying.

Bellda smiled at the sweet old lady who reminded her of her late grandmother, as she wiped away her tears with the sleeve of her sweater.

"Yes, ma'am. I'm okay," Bellda spoke.

"Whatever it is, baby, you just ask God for deliverance, and he will give it to you, okay?" the black woman in her late sixties but with the energy of a twenty-five-year-old said.

Bellda could tell that the lady had been gorgeous in her prime, and that she was a devoted Christian, as evidenced by the gold cross around her neck.

I need a man to treat me queenly. Fuck being a sideline bitch! Bellda wanted to say, but refrained from it and simply thanked her. "Thank you, ma'am. I will do that."

"Ma'am, you're next in line," the store clerk said to Bellda, who hadn't realized that the line had moved.

"Yes, ma'am," Bellda said as she walked to the checkout counter to pay for her shoes.

"That's $49.99, ma'am."

I can't let him keep doing this to me, Bellda thought while she waited for her credit card to clear.

Beep!

"It's all good. Thank you for shopping at Sketchers, ma'am," the unattractive blonde said, cutting her eyes at Bellda.

Bellda smiled and then kindly said, "You're welcome, ugly," as she walked out of the store.

On her way out, she passed by a jewelry booth and a scintillating *XO* necklace caught her eye, prolonging her plans of leaving. She just had to stop and check out the necklace.

Damn! That bitch got some diamonds on her! she thought as she admired the dazzling necklace.

"How much for that *X* and *O* necklace?" Bellda asked the

Arab clerk.

"This one? Ahhh, it's my favorite, and I'm sure it'll look very nice on you, gorgeous," the man said while going inside the glass counter to retrieve the piece of jewelry.

Bellda noticed that the Arab was about her age and that he was handsome as well. But picturing herself with him was halted quickly, since she never had dated anyone outside her race before.

"This one is costly!" he said honestly. He whistled, which made Bellda laugh from the face he made.

"Boy, let me see how much it is."

"How 'bout trying it on first to see if you like the feel of it. Come, turn around!" the Arab clerk said, gesturing a circular motion with his finger for Bellda to turn around.

"Sure," Bellda retorted as she turned around to allow him to clasp the necklace behind her neck.

Bellda never saw the attentive eyes of a man who was strutting toward her.

"Take a look!" the clerk said, spinning around a mirror so Bellda could see for herself.

When Bellda looked in the mirror and saw the man standing behind her, who she hadn't noticed watching her from a distance, she was startled and almost jumped out of her skin.

"Oh shit!" she shouted at the handsome man behind her.

"Sorry, beautiful. You look nice with that blinging-ass necklace on. It was so bright, I just had to come see who it was."

"You sure it's not from all them damn golds in yo' mouth! Nigga, you can't be doing that. I could have shot yo' ass!" Bellda told the handsome man, almost forgetting she still had the necklace on.

"Oh shit, sorry!" Bellda said, turning around to return the necklace to the Arab clerk while Mr. Handsome eyed down her phat ass.

In nurse scrubs, Bellda still was a bad bitch, and Mr. Handsome was pleased with every detail of her curves accentuated by her baby-blue scrubs.

"How much is it?" Bellda asked for the price.

"For you, $9,500!"

"What?" Bellda exclaimed.

"Hey, the original price was $10,000. So being that you're such a gorgeous woman, I cut it down."

"Boy, do it look like I have that type of money?" she asked.

"Then that means that the right nigga isn't in your life," the handsome man responded.

Oh no he didn't! Bellda thought, ready to accost the handsome nigga and stand her ground.

But when she snaked her neck over him, the sight of him peeling off straight Benjamins from a phat wad left her dumbstruck.

"Put that necklace back on her neck. I just want to pay for it just to sit on her neck," Mr. Handsome said, still counting and licking his fingers.

I'm fucking the biggest dope boy on the Treasure Coast, and I can't even purchase a $9,500 necklace, but I bet his wife could. Fuck Pat! Bellda thought, not realizing that she was crying again.

"Baby, whatever it is that got you hurt, just know I'm not one of those flashy niggas. I know a real woman when I see one," the handsome man said as he was paying the necklace in full. "Just call me when you get a chance, beautiful, and we can talk about anything—and I mean anything."

"You don't even know my name, boy!" Bellda said.

"Of course I do. Your name is Bellda Success, according to your CNA name tag," Mr. Handsome retorted, pointing at her ID card clipped on the V-neck of her scrubs top.

When Bellda looked down at her tag, she smiled, blushed a bit, and then said, "Oh!" She then said, "And what is your name?" while watching him write down his number on the back of the receipt for the necklace.

"My name is Real, but you can call me Jermaine. Now hit me up when you get a chance and are ready for me to take you out somewhere nice," he said as he walked off, leaving Bellda and the Arab speechless.

"Damn! He's fine as hell and on time!" Bellda exclaimed.

"Yes, he is beautiful, and if I was you, I'd go see what type of car he's getting into," the clerk said, with a lot of femininity in his voice, which prompted Bellda to take a second look at him. When she did, she saw it clear as day.

"Are you by chance a homo?" Bellda inquired.

"No, baby. I'm the rainbow!" the Arab clerk said with a flick of his wrist.

"Oh, hell no!" Bellda exclaimed, laughing as she stormed off with her $9,500 necklace and Mr. Jermaine's number.

Damn! That nigga is fine. I'ma give him a couple days. I don't need him thinkin' that I'm like any of these easy-to-go bitches in Martin County, Bellda thought as she drove away from the mall in her Lexus truck that Pat had bought her last year.

* * *

As Real drove through East Stuart to meet up with T-Gutta, he couldn't stop thinking about the bad bitch Bellda.

He knew that she wasn't a gold-digging bitch, because when he had left her standing at the jewelry booth, she didn't call out for him or follow him out of the mall. Bellda had no clue that she had scored so high in his book.

After leaving the mall, he pulled her up as soon as he could to see who she was. Seeing that she was single made him even more eager to get to know her, with a little skepticism of her being so beautiful but without a man. She was from the Stuart area, and if she was a ho, T-Gutta would definitely know. T-Gutta had fucked so many hos in the lowly populated Stuart area and Martin County that he lost count years ago.

Real pulled into the driveway of T-Gutta's baby mama, LeLe's, house and honked his horn twice.

A couple seconds later, T-Gutta strutted outside dressed in all-black attire. He walked to the passenger side of Real's brand new BMW truck. He was smiling and showing off his new platinum grill that sparkled ominously in his mouth.

"What's up, nigga?" T-Gutta asked as he hopped inside while smoking a phat dro blunt.

"You tell me! I see you done went and upgraded on me with the platinum, nigga."

"Something like that," T-Gutta retorted.

"Check it. Do you know this bitch right here?" Real asked, wasting no time getting to his reason for coming to see T-Gutta.

"Hell yeah! That's phat booty Bellda, dirty. She lives in Salerno, brah, and she's definitely single," T-Gutta explained.

"What you mean single?" Real inquired.

"Ain't no nigga 'round here hittin' that bitch, but she tight with my baby mama," T-Gutta retorted.

"Who, LeLe?" Real asked.

"She's the only baby mama I got. She Zoe too," T-Gutta

stated.

"Bellda?" Real questioned.

"Yeah! She Zoe, brah. Like I said, if she has a nigga, he ain't from 'round Martin County. So, to the public's eyes, she's single," T-Gutta added.

Shorty too damn bad to not have a nigga somewhere in her life. If she did, I know the nigga's not treating her good. She cried in front of me, and them were tears of pain. She's hurt, and like any hurt soul that needs to be rescued, she's highly vulnerable. She needs a real nigga to come treat her like a queen. I gotta see what lil baby 'bout, even if it's just one night. That phat ass got my name on it, just callin' my name! Real said to himself while deep in thought.

T-Gutta took the moment of silence as Real searching his mind for more questions about Bellda while he stared out the window and watched two boys toss a football.

"So, she from Salerno, huh?" Real inquired about the city in Martin County that had a hood called 46th Avenue.

"Yeah. She lives out there with her dad, brah!"

"What street?"

"Innez," T-Gutta responded. "Nigga, what's up? You must done ran across the bitch or something."

"Yeah, I caught her at the mall an hour ago, feel me. Dat bitch is definitely swole back there too," Real exclaimed.

"Hell yeah, she is," T-Gutta agreed, exhaling smoke from his mouth.

"Shit still hot, T-Gutta! So, play it safe out here, feel me?" Real told him.

"Yeah, I got ya, brah."

"Well, I'ma get up with ya later, brah," Real said as he threw the gear into drive.

"You know where I'm at, brah," T-Gutta said, bumping fists with Real.

"Be careful, Gutta," Real reminded.

"Trust me, brah, I will," T-Gutta said as he lifted up his shirt, showing Real his Glock .40. "This bitch ready fo' whatever," he said as he exited the SUV and walked back inside.

Real sat for a few minutes staring at Bellda's Facebook profile picture. At that moment, he wanted Bellda to be in the same vicinity as him.

I'ma get shorty fo' real. Real committed himself to the task ahead of him. He then pulled out of T-Gutta's driveway, engrossed in all types of different approaches he could step up with Bellda. He chose the gentleman route.

Maybe she could be wifey? Hell nah, nigga! You got too much shit on yo' plate to be worried 'bout making a bitch yo' wife! Real reminded himself.

Chapter Ten

Port-au-Prince, Haiti

When Polo Mindor was in his hometown, his presence was always known. There was always a celebration when he was in town. If Polo ran for president, he knew beyond a doubt that he would be elected. He was very compassionate when it came to his hometown. He took care of the homeless and supported educational funds so kids could have a chance to become the people they dreamed of becoming in life.

He sat in the backseat of the luxurious, all-black armored Mercedes. As he watched the kids run alongside the car, waving their hands at the man they waited to see each month, it warmed Polo's heart. It was the same home he shared with Black, whom he prayed to catch slipping, although the gods would never allow them both to spill each other's blood in their homeland. Sitting beside him was his lethal yet trustworthy hit man, who Black presumed to be dead: Bo-Bo.

They were home to visit Polo's 105-year-old grandmother, Ms. Benita. She was a reputable voodoo priestess. Ms. Benita was a powerful woman who could tell the past, present, and future with her eyes closed. She not only foretold an individual's future, but she could also heal the sick and curse the wicked. No other priestess was known to be as powerful, for she was a mutual translator, which allowed her to mingle with the ancient gods.

She lived alone and peacefully in the dark confines of her shack in the heart of the gutta. She was protected by an army of village soldiers who adapted to the city under her spell.

"Polo, Polo! Polo!" the kids shouted outside the Mercedes.

They were running alongside his car, excited to see him again. He held an AK-47 rifle on his lap, with his finger on the trigger, the same as Bo-Bo. Although he was home in the crowded streets, he still had to be ready for warfare. Black had his men everywhere, including their hometown of Port-au-Prince.

"Slow down, give me a moment with the kids," Polo commanded his chauffeur, who immediately slowed the car from fifteen to ten miles per hour.

Polo gingerly looked at his surroundings to check for any activity or movement that was amiss. He waited until he was between a small abandoned building and fruit stand before he decided to halt the car. "Okay, stop here!" he instructed in Creole.

As soon as the car came to a stop, Polo pressed a button to roll down his window. Bo-Bo paid close attention to their surroundings. Behind his dark shades, he could clearly see everyone.

"Polo! Polo!" the kids continued to call out his name.

He smiled at the brave, bare-chested muscular boys who were around the ages of eleven. He could remember a time when he and Black had been so elated to see a drug lord named Pete come home from the States and shower the streets of Haiti with his love.

"Polo! Polo!" the shouts of a dozen or more kids grew intensely.

Polo pulled out a phat wad of cash from his Armani slacks and began peeling off sets of $300 and passing them out to each of the boys.

"Go give that to Mama, and tell her Polo gave it to her to feed the family," he told every boy to whom he handed money.

When they got the money, they thanked him and ran off to do exactly what Polo asked of them.

"Thank you, Polo. We love you!" the kids exclaimed, highly gratified.

A little girl around the age of eleven caught his eye. She was standing behind the rowdy boys. She had a filthy face, tattered clothing, and a dirty doll in her arms. She had a streak of tears cascading down her face. Blood instantly began to pour slowly from her nose. Polo quickly concluded that the girl was very ill.

"Come here," he told the girl in Creole as he waved the excited boys to the side.

The little girl slowly walked toward him, badly trembling and taking baby steps.

That is when Polo saw the bump on her stomach beneath her filthy dress and then the flashing red light.

"Go! Go! Go!" Polo screamed while rolling up his window in panic.

The Mercedes tires spun and burned rubber while attempting to flee from the danger.

Boom!

The explosion erupted loudly and shook the entire city, sending a tremendous load of blood and body organs onto the car, which was still intact due to the armor.

The Mercedes was finally able to flee the gruesome sight. Where gleeful children had just stood together excited to see Polo, they were now all dead.

"Damn it! Damn it! Damn it!" Polo cried as he pounded his fist hard on the window.

"Fuck!" Bo-Bo exclaimed, shaken from the aftermath.

"She was a little girl, man!" Polo shouted angrily.

The chauffeur continued on his way to their destination, speeding through the streets of Haiti, until he halted in front of Ms. Benita's shack.

"We're here, boss!" the chauffeur spoke in Creole, without looking back at his upset boss.

Polo unabashedly dried his eyes with the towel he kept around his neck to wipe off the persistent sweat from his face caused by the extremely high temperature in Haiti.

When he went to look out the window, all Polo could see was the gruesome aftermath of the explosion. The excessive splatter of blood and guts made it impossible for him clearly to see through the window to check his surroundings. Although he knew without a doubt that danger couldn't come anywhere near Ms. Benita's vicinity due to her village soldiers and protection spells, he was still prompted to move with precaution.

"Check it out, Haitian!" Polo ordered his chauffeur, who quickly exited the car and looked carefully for any signs of trouble.

When he saw none, he opened the bloody door with a towel and allowed Polo to step outside. He shielded Polo and escorted him inside his grandmother's shack. He passed her men holding AK-47s, with Bo-Bo on his heels, walking backward and keeping an eye for any sight of their enemies, with his own AK-47 swinging from side to side. They were taking no chances.

* * *

"It's time fo' yo' ass to get home, Joc. I ain't playing' with you either, nigga!" Lala shouted over the phone to Joc, who was inside Jake's store getting his dick sucked by Keshia in the restroom.

Despite her getting her ass torn out by Lala, Keshia was still creeping with Lala's baby daddy.

"I told you I'll be home in a few. I'm doin' something right now," Joc said sluggishly as he took a swig from his bottle of Budweiser.

"Where are you, Joc?"

"I'm makin' money," Joc retorted while watching Keshia suck on his balls and artistically stroke his large dick.

Damn! This bitch can suck a dick! Joc thought.

"Joc, you have an hour to get here, nigga. I swear to God I'ma come lookin' fo' you," Lala said sternly. "And when I find you, it won't be nice either," she threatened.

"Baby, I'm coming, okay!" Joc exclaimed as he hung up the phone while shooting his load down Keshia's gullet and watching her swallow every drop. "Damn!" Joc exclaimed while holding onto the back of her head.

Keshia cleaned him up thoroughly and then tucked him back into his Boss jeans. When she came up from her knees, she looked herself over in the dingy rusty mirror. Joc admired her and lustfully wanted to pull down her black tights, bend her over the filthy sink, and fuck her hard from the back, just like he had done innumerable times in the same restroom. But he knew he couldn't do it since she was on her period.

"Well, daddy, I guess you better get home before somebody beat yo' ass!" Keshia said, fanning out her golden dreadlocks.

Smack!

Joc slapped Keshia's succulent backside, unable to resist touching her enormous ass.

"Boy, we have an entire week. Don't make it hard on yourself. Now let's go 'cause it's hot in this shit, and I'm burning up!" Keshia said while wiping her neck with a napkin that she had pulled from a napkin holder.

"Alright, let's go!" Joc said as he walked out of the restroom and down the dark hallway, with Keshia on his heels.

"God damn it! I swear y'all muthafuckas done went over y'all's time. Where is my extra fee at?" Jake asked Joc and Keshia as they walked up from the restroom.

"Shut up, Jake. We was not dat long," Keshia said with a smirk on her face as she ran out of the front door in a hurry.

"Yeah! Dat's why yo' ass running," Jake said to her as she hit the door.

"Shut up, Jake!" Keshia said again, letting the door slam behind her.

"She runnin' 'cause she thinks Lala's ass on her way up here."

"Oh, is that so?" Jake said to Joc while peeling $300 off a wad for watching out for him and Keshia.

"Bet dat up, nigga. Now go! I got a game to look at," Jake said, getting back to his NBA game on his portable television.

"Lebron's ass goin' home, nigga. He can't do it by himself," Joc said to Jake.

"What! You got Curry suckin' yo dick too?" Jake retorted, causing Joc to erupt into laughter as he continued out the front door.

When Joc stepped outside in the chilly air, he saw his homeboy Meat Head standing out in the open by the store's disconnected pay phone serving a friend.

Dat's how muthafuckas catch a drug case, being muthafuckin' careless, Joc thought as he walked toward this gray box Chevy sitting on twenty-eight-inch rims.

It was 2:00 a.m., and despite the block still being hot from Popa Zoe's murder, shit was still running fast on the money tip. When Joc saw the black Mercury sitting at the corner, he first thought it was the police, until he saw the twenty-six-inch rims on the ride.

Damn, who is dat? Joc wanted to know, unable to make out the driver behind the tints.

The car made a slow right toward Jake's store and crept slow, and that's when Joc became alert. He quickly made a dash for his car to retrieve his big .357, but the moment he made it to the locked door and got the key in, shots erupted from the passenger side.

Boom! Boom! Boom! Boom! Boom!

The shots hit Joc, instantly dropping him. Meat Head tried to scramble away, but he was shot in his legs, disabling him from walking or running.

B-Zoe jumped out of the Mercury passenger side with this Mossberg pump and ran up to Joc, who had taken shots to his side but was still breathing.

"Death comes like da thief in da night, nigga! Smile for da reaper!" B-Zoe said as he then pumped two slugs into Joc's face, leaving him disfigured and lifeless.

The two fiends who were in the darkness stayed where they were and watched the entire hit go down. B-Zoe ran toward Meat Head, who was crawling yet trying to get away, but to no avail.

"Give me a name, nigga, or you die!" B-Zoe said while aiming his pump at Meat Head.

"Man, I don't know what you talkin' 'bout!" Meat Head exclaimed, wincing in pain from his shattered legs.

"Oh yeah? So dis how we gonna die, huh?" B-Zoe said as he pumped two slugs into the back of Meat Head's scalp.

Boom! Boom!

B-Zoe quickly hopped back into the car and then sped off the moment he sat down.

When Jake heard the tires peel out, he ran out of the store with his .357 in hand and immediately saw Joc, slain by his car, and Meat Head slain on the sidewalk.

"Lord have mercy! Damn, Joc!" Jake cried out as he rushed back inside to call 911.

* * *

Polo sat hypnotized on a comfortable throne-looking chair at the candlelit table, with his eyes closed. He was nude and wore a necklace of bloody chicken bones while his grandmother Benita recited her ritual tongues in Creole. She was also nude and wearing bloody chicken bones around her neck and over her sagging breasts. Pierced through her large, dark nipples was a set of black beads that fell to the ground. She was an extremely dark woman who stood five three and was a hefty 230 pounds.

"Grandson, a powerful man will soon come," she spoke in Creole as she walked around the table toward Polo.

She removed the chicken bones from around his neck and then placed a necklace of black beads and a brown pouch as a charm. Inside the pouch were the ashes of Polo's grandfather, who was a voodoo priest as well before he died at 101 years old.

"You shall overcome your enemy and stop him in his wrath. Oh, grandson, there surely will be wrath. But don't be afraid. You shall overcome," Grandma Benita warned Polo of her vision.

"Who sent the girl?" Polo asked unconsciously with his

eyes closed.

"Who killed the little girl? She was eleven years old. She was sent to kill you by your enemy, Polo. Black is a heartless man who's protected by the gods as well. He failed when he sent the little diseased girl from her shack to kill you. She was a sacrifice for the gods. The men still are lingering in a shack. I see four of them alone!"

"Where, Grandma?" Polo desperately asked.

Grandma Benita smiled as she drew a bloody circle on his forehead inside a bloody hexagon. It was the blood of a cat and a sheep combined. She was casting a protection spell upon him.

"Down by the little barn," she began in a hypnotic state, "you'll see a shack with very drunk men. There are four of them. You will hear them speak blasphemously of a powerful man, Polo," Grandmother Benita said.

She then snapped her finger, awaking Polo from his trance. A moment ago, she was hearing the confines of Polo's heart before he came to her shack. He had no clue that he knew exactly where to find the assassins; however, he never would have known consciously.

* * *

Polo and Bo-Bo left Grandmother Benita's shack and hopped in the backseat of another armored vehicle. It was a smoke-gray Hummer with dark tints, and it had a submachine gun attached to the hood.

"Take me to the little barn, Haitian," Polo demanded his driver.

"Yes, sir," the chauffeur responded.

When they pulled up to the section called Little Barn, he racked his AK-47 rifle and then looked over at Bo-Bo, who firmly held onto his.

"Let's go!" Polo said as they exited the Hummer.

Bo-Bo followed suit as they quietly passed by peaceful shacks with inhabitants who appeared to be asleep.

Polo turned right onto a filthy strip of a dirt road and saw black cats scramble everywhere. They stayed on the road for a short time and then meticulously turned left. As he walked in the direction of the shack, to which he was unconsciously determined to reach, he and Bo-Bo heard gleeful laughter. Polo stopped in his tracks when he heard his name followed by another round of laughter and blasphemies in Creole.

"Come," he told Bo-Bo as they continued until they stood in front of the shack with the tan door.

As more laughter erupted, Polo kicked down the feeble door, catching the men sitting at a wooden table off guard. Polo and Bo-Bo released a deadly fusillade at his enemies. All the men caught slipping were left bullet-riddled and lifeless.

"No man can kill Polo. Tell Black and his gods that Polo cannot die!" Polo shouted in rage as he then released an extended clip of fifty on all four of Black's Haitians. "Zo'pound, muthafuckas!" he screamed, with an impish smirk on his face.

Chapter Eleven

"**N**o! How the fuck y'all gonna let this happen? That's my fuckin' baby daddy!" Lala cried hysterically while being held back by Martin County deputies.

Her shrill was heartbreaking, and the deputies understood her pain.

"Ma'am, we can't let you come 'cross the line," a sheriff's deputy said to her.

He was a black man in his twenties and one of the first to arrive at the chilling scene. Yellow tape had been set up around Jake's store's porch. Both Joc and Meat Head's bodies were covered in white shrouds. The entire block was lit up like Christmas, with a crowd of grieving family and friends for both victims.

Meat Head's mother had been rushed to the hospital when the devastating news came knocking at her front door.

"I can't believe this! Please bring him back!" Lala continued to shrill.

It took Lala's mother and other Ms. Gorgeouses to come pull her away as they all cried uncontrollably.

Real, Shamoney, and Lunatic pulled up an hour later to the crowded block and saw that Joc and Meat Head's bodies were still on the scene.

Damn! Real thought as he looked on at the aftermath of what without a doubt came behind hitting Popa Zoe.

After Jake had called 911, he called Real with the devastating news that they had lost two swamp niggas.

"Man! What we gonna do? Play like these Zoes ain't do dis shit!" a swamp nigga named Var exclaimed, wiping away his tears with his black T-shirt.

"Hell no. We ain't gonna play like they ain't do this shit!" Real said to Var, embracing his homeboy and consoling him. "We gonna get these muthafuckas, brah. We gonna get 'em!" Real promised.

When he looked farther into the crowd of people, he made eye contact with Lala and could see the pain on her face. He knew Lala loved Joc to some point, and she was transparently showing him how vast her love was for him, despite them cheating on each other. It was something Real didn't want to be a part of. There was no way he was going to be a rebound nigga to replace a dead man.

"Man, I gotta get up from here," Var said, breaking away from Real and walking away from the scene.

"When dis shit clears out, we runnin' in on all these Zoe traps and gettin' them out of our hood and county," Real told Shamoney, who concisely nodded his head in agreement.

* * *

Detective Mark Harris was a veteran of the Martin County Homicide Department, and what he hated most was being perplexed when solving a murder. He was a fifty-five-year-old black man who stood six three and weighed 212 pounds. He was solid, with salt-and-pepper hair. His partner, Det. Lisa Holmes, was a strikingly gorgeous, thirty-five-year-old blonde woman who stood five five and weighed 140 pounds. She was just as perplexed at the scene.

"First the Haitians and now this! What connection do we have?" Det. Harris asked Holmes, who stood near her unmarked car with her hands resting on her hips close to her Glock 21.

"I'd say we maybe have something, but why?" she asked, perplexed.

"Lisa, I just don't get this one," Harris retorted as he walked back under the yellow tape to thoroughly investigate the crime.

With a gloved hand, Harris knelt down to where Joc's body was and pulled back the shroud to inspect the nature of the wounds, praying that they could tell him a story he hadn't heard, or provide a clue to solve the case. But unfortunately, there was no luck on that hope.

"A Mossberg pump for sure!" Lisa said over Harris's shoulder while looking down at Joc's disfigured face.

"Yep," Harris retorted, then covered Joc's face and stood up.

"This one really scares me, Lisa," Harris admitted.

"Tell me about it," she replied.

* * *

"So, do you think Shamoney is responsible for Popa Zoe?" Black asked Pat on his iPhone while pacing in his spacious, opulent living room.

"Honestly, Black, no. I do think that one of them niggas in the swamp is behind it," Pat admitted.

"B-Zoe did a good job. Who did he have with him?" Black inquired.

"He took one of his men with him."

"Was he paid in full?" Black asked.

"Yeah, everything!" Pat replied.

"Okay, dat's good business," Black added.

"Haitian mafia will always be good business, brah!" Pat said.

"Always. You know that Polo got away again? Da nigga is swift."

"Tell me about it," Pat said in Creole.

"He killed all my men from Little Barn. No one knows how he knew it was them. Some say Grandma Benita, and we all know if she had any vision, then it was her," Black explained.

"So, tell me dis," Pat began, but paused.

Black could hear a woman screaming in the background. No doubt it was Gina.

"Black, she's going into labor, brah! Oh shit!" Pat was exhilarated.

"Congrats, boy! Go attend to her. We'll talk later," Black said as he hung up the phone.

Black lived alone in his mansion, other than his guards outside. Since his wife had died, he never remarried and only dealt with women when he was sexually frustrated. When he did get a hold of some pussy, it was always a threesome.

I think I'ma call up them twins. Shit! A nigga love seeing them bitches go at it, Black thought while calling up his main bodyguard, Choppa.

"Yo," Choppa answered into the phone.

"I need them Jamaican twins," Black said to him, and Choppa then hung up the phone.

Black walked upstairs to his room and stripped down to nothing and hopped into bed. While he awaited the twins' arrival, all he could think about was his swift nemesis, Polo.

One day you will not be able to escape my wrath. Soon, I will have your chump ass, nigga! Black thought, engrossed in vengeance. *One day, muthafucka, I will have you!* he thought, never foreseeing the real threat that was approaching him.

Twenty minutes had passed before the twins entered the room wearing nothing but their birthday suits. They lustrously sashayed over to Black and climbed in bed on both sides of him. Their names were Keke and Meme, and both had a swarthy complexion. They stood equal at five eight, with Coke-bottle frames and stallion thighs. They were definitely eye candy from Opa-locka, Miami, and were *Smooth Girl* models.

Meme took Black's erect dick into her mouth while Keke climbed on top of his face.

"That's right, baby. Put dat pussy in me face!" Black said in his best English as he began sucking on her throbbing clitoris.

He then grabbed her succulent ass with both palms and ate out her hairless phat pussy like he was eating a juicy watermelon.

"Uhhh! Yes, daddy! Eat dis phat pussy, mon!" Keke purred as she seductively gyrated her hips and rode his face. "Yes, daddy! Uhhh!" Keke then moaned while sister took Black's dick deep down her throat without gagging on his enormous size and girth.

Clap! Clap!

Keke clapped her hands, and Keith Sweat came softly pouring from the hidden surround system, adding spice to their grooves.

The Haitian dream. Fuck the American dream! Every Haitian needs them two bitches by law, Black thought as he fucked Keke with his tongue.

Chapter Twelve

A couple days after Joc and Meat Head's murder, every nigga from the swamp who knew how to shed blood showed up at Shamoney's crib in Port St. Lucie and got broke off with exactly what needed to be done.

"V-Money, Var, and Alleycat, y'all three will hit the trap on 3rd Street, while Bruna, Shamoney, and Ham hit the trap on 2nd Street. Me, Lunatic, and T-Gutta, we gonna take the Westbrook trap. I don't care if a baby is cryin', take that shit down," Real directed everyone.

Everyone hung out in the den, where the pool table was stacked with various types of submachine guns and assault rifles.

"We 'bout to make these Zoes respect Martin County thoroughly. Fuck playing with 'em!" Real exclaimed.

"We ain't stoppin' 'til our niggas hit dat dirt. And then when they covered, we'll still gonna bring pressure to these Zoes. Anything that looks like a Zoe, we'll whack his ass. No hesitation," Real continued.

Every nigga in the room was attentive and ready to show the Haitians how real shit could get.

"Man, you ain't gotta worry 'bout Var hesitating," Var sincerely expressed.

Var stood five eleven and weighed 210 pounds. He was a straight head bussa, who was very humble, and Real knew beyond any doubt that he would be the last nigga to worry about hesitating. Everyone in the room knew how close Var was to Joc.

"Man, we gonna make these crackas' job hard and bloody," said Johnny, who was going on another mission while the swamp was being raided.

Johnny and his ace, Su'Rabbit, would be kicking down doors in Stuart.

"Let's remember, tonight is about our fallen soldiers and, most definitely, for their families. Let's make this shit hit the world news. Fuck the local news, my niggas!" Real announced, throwing his chromed AK-47 rifle about his head in the air.

"Hell yeah!" everyone shrilled together.

"Then let's do this shit!" Real exclaimed as he racked his AK-47.

* * *

The havoc that was occurring a mile down the road left Kentucky worried for his boy Real. He had been in lockdown for one week now under an inmate murder investigation. When the detectives, the inspector of the DOC, and the warden had questioned him, Kentucky told them that he had no idea what had happened in his cell out of his presence, and then he remained quiet. He knew that they wouldn't be able to pin the murders on him without a witness—and that they didn't have.

Kentucky was sure there were inmates out on the compound ready to give him up, but with Chucky on the compound, no one would dare risk their life. Kentucky had lost a phone and a couple ounces of K2 because his mattress was in a crime lab somewhere being tested for DNA. He regretted not thinking more intelligently.

His cellmate was a resident of Martin County and happened to be from Real's hood, and he knew Real well. His name was Skeetmeat, and he was receiving the Stuart newspaper every other day. That's where Kentucky had read the story of the sudden murders in Indiantown a mile down the road from the prison. All Kentucky did was work on his novels while Skeetmeat read his collection of urban novels.

"So, you ready to work out?" Kentucky asked Skeetmeat, who was deeply engrossed in a Terri Woods novel titled *Dutch*.

Kentucky continued to keep at his daily workout to stay in good shape. He refused to be out of shape when it was time for any split-second opportunity to be taken advantage of. Every day he worked out, he saw it as planning a great escape.

"Yeah, I'll push with ya. Just let me finish this chapter," Skeetmeat replied, deeply engrossed in the Terri Woods novel.

"Alright, we'll push in a couple more minutes," Kentucky retorted as he stood up from the bottom bunk and began to warm up for the intense workout.

Kentucky walked to the cell door and looked out into the wing and downstairs from the top tier. He caught his homeboy Guru's skinny ass doing push-ups.

"Guru, yo' skinny ass still the same size. But I gotta give it to you, yo' ass be goin' hard!" Kentucky screamed down to Guru in cell 5 downstairs.

"Stop hatin' on a nigga! I'll outdo yo' phat ass, boy!" Guru shouted back.

"Get the fuck off the door, cell 5!" Lockdown Sgt. Gaskin yelled out to Guru, who was in a cell alone and classified as a troublesome inmate.

"Cracka, fuck you and yo' door!" Guru spat back at the sergeant.

"You just love getting gassed, huh?" Sgt. Gaskin asked, standing in front of Guru's cell door, challenging him.

Every inmate in the wing knew that Guru didn't give a fuck about getting hit with any form of restraint chemicals. He was used to it and loved making a show for other inmates.

"Cracka, you know I don't see no gas. Bitch, let's run this shit. I dare you, cracka. Go ahead and open my hatch and watch me eat that shit like candy, cracka!" Guru said to Sgt. Gaskin, who began laughing because he knew that Guru was a gas freak.

"Any other day I'd spray the black off yo' skinny ass, but today is my Friday, and paperwork is not what I want to do," Sgt. Gaskin backed down.

"The only color coming off of me is from when yo' wife sucking my dick until the skin comes off!" Guru said, causing the entire wing to erupt into laughter and the sergeant's face to turn a rosy red.

"Don't worry, Tisdale," Gaskin said, shaking his head, "I'll have the last laugh come Monday."

"What you gonna do, go home and grow some dick and balls, cracka?" Guru said, getting another round of laughter out of the inmates on the wing, humiliating Sgt. Gaskins. "Damn, Sergeant! What, you embarrassed now?" Guru continued to verbally abuse Sgt. Gaskin, who walked off further into the wing, trying to catch an inmate on the door with something to lose.

Guru was going home next month on his max out, so there wasn't shit that Gaskin could do to harm him. A write-up for disrespect would only be a joke. Unfortunately for Sgt. Gaskin, he was unable to find an inmate because they all got off the door to avoid sticking out like a sore thumb. When the sergeant looked up and saw Kentucky on the door, he thought about making an example of him, but he realized that he too had nothing to lose. Kentucky had three life sentences running wild.

What the fuck could I do to Spears? The man has more life than a newborn baby, Sergeant Gaskin thought as he walked back to his officer station.

* * *

Gina cried as she held her adorable seven-pound baby boy, who she had given birth to only hours ago. She named him Patron, after his daddy, despite knowing deep down that there was a strong possibility of the little boy not being Pat's. But she would never tell him or Shamoney, who she had been sleeping with behind Pat's back. She was grateful that the baby strongly favored her, and she had yet to see the baby open his eyes to determine whose eyes he had.

"Looks like you robbed me on the genes, baby," Pat said while looking down at his son, who looked so much like his mother.

"I guess I was on top puttin' in all the work," Gina said as she then kissed Pat on his lips.

"I love you, beautiful," Pat sincerely told his wife, a woman he wouldn't leave for any other woman in the world, not even his gorgeous mistress, Bellda.

"I love you too, daddy," Gina retorted as her nurse walked into the room.

"Sorry if I'm interrupting the making of another baby," Nurse Vanessa said while looking at Pat and Gina engrossed in each other's moonstruck stares.

Gina and Pat both laughed together at Vanessa's comment.

"Woman, we have at least six weeks to do that."

"Girl, who you talking to? That's what the protocol says, not the mind, heart, and desire to break the protocol," Vanessa said while taking Gina's vitals.

Vanessa was a heavy-set pecan-brown woman in her late thirties, as opposed to Gina, who was in her late twenties. She compassionately cared for Gina during her labor, and Gina thoroughly appreciated her kindness. She would see that Vanessa received a phat check for overdoing her duty.

Damn! I got me a handsome little boy. I got to really consider slowing down out here, Pat thought, knowing that he was too deep in the game to consider backing out. Black needed him.

* * *

It was 3:15 a.m., and despite the swamp being on fire with the police roaming, Real and his crew were gratified to see that the swamp was dead. Real circled the block in Westbrook, a small section in the swamp, and parked at the community Boys & Girls Club.

"We gonna take the rest on foot," Real said as he killed the engine on his SUV, "and come up the back way."

"What? We gonna come up the canal?" Lunatic asked.

"Yeah!" Real retorted.

"You don't think ol' man John is out lurking," Lunatic asked, concerned about the Jamaican who never came out during the day and lived in complete darkness.

"Shit! If he intervenes in any kind of way, he'll get it too," Real said.

"I know that's right!" T-Gutta added from the backseat.

"Let's go, my nigga!" Real said as they exited the SUV on foot.

The trio quickly walked to the canal and traveled west, being furtive while holding AK-47s in their hands. Real carried a backpack with four Molotov cocktails inside. The canal led them behind folks' backyards, which stirred a couple of dogs, which began barking at the creeping trio.

When Real came to the Haitians' house, he, Lunatic, and T-Gutta leaped over the short gate. Although the house looked deserted with all the inside lights off, Real knew better than to underestimate the eerie darkness.

"Man, this shit looks crazy, dirty," T-Gutta spoke in a whisper.

The trio hid behind a tool shed, which they used as a shield.

"Yeah, it do! Maybe they're waiting. What you say, Real?" Lunatic asked in a hushed voice.

"There's only one way to find out, my nigga!" Real said as he took the backpack off his shoulders, unzipped it, and dug inside to retrieve the Molotov cocktails and a lighter. "Either way it goes down, these Haitians got to get the fuck out of the swamp!" Real said. "Y'all two niggas cover me while I throw them inside."

Lunatic and T-Gutta both racked their AK-47s in unison and spoke together, "We got you!"

Real meticulously lit one cocktail and then ignited the other with the already burning first one. He swiftly and nimbly ran from behind the tool shed and then hurled the cocktails into a bedroom and den window. All hell broke loose!

Chop! Chop! Chop! Chop!

"Yeah, bitch! Let's get it!" Real shouted as fire exchanged between the Haitians and his two compadres who were holding him down.

Real ran behind the shed and grabbed his backpack with the last two cocktails, along with his AK-47. The fusillade continued between the Haitians and his two compadres. Real played the Haitians and used the darkness to his advantage by quickly running on the opposite side of the gunfire.

When he made it to the side of the house, he lit one of the cocktails and hurled it into another bedroom. He then ran to the front of the house, where he caught three men trying to creep out a side door. Real took all of them down to their deaths and then lit the last Molotov cocktail and tossed it into the open door. The four-bedroom trap house was raging with flames, and soon the shooting from inside ceased. When three more Haitians attempted to flee out the front door of the fire-engulfed house, Real took them down one by one.

Chop! Chop! Chop! Chop!

He almost turned the AK-47 on T-Gutta and Lunatic when they came running alongside the burning house. From the looks of the home, there couldn't be a living soul inside unless it was Satan himself. At that conclusion, the trio successfully fled the scene.

* * *

On 3rd and 2nd Streets, the rest of the team had successfully completed their tasks, leaving the trap houses burning and the Haitian men slain. The trap houses were officially gone from the swamp, just as Real had planned.

In East Stuart, true menaces to society Johnny and Su'Rabbit had successfully run into the Haitian trap houses and laid everyone down. Four were dead, while T-Zoe was still breathing. T-Zoe was the driver of the black Mercury and one of Pat's good hit men. He was also Shamoney's archenemy and B-Zoe's codefendant from the night he killed Joc and Meat Head, so he was sure to pay for it.

When T-Zoe saw himself ambushed by the two masked men, he surrendered and gave up all the dope and money.

Su'Rabbit stood five four and weighed two hundred pounds. He was solid, with a dark-brown complexion and a mouthful of golds. He was an old-school nigga and mentor to Johnny, who was old enough to be Su'Rabbit's son. It was his decision not to kill T-Zoe and to bring him along for Real to deal with, and Su'Rabbit subsequently beat the truth out of him about B-Zoe's mission. T-Zoe was frightened, and he gave up B-Zoe like a machine returned change for a dollar.

"You want to live, then you better let us know everything we need to know 'bout this nigga named B-Zoe!" Su'Rabbit informed T-Zoe, who was face down and bloody on the kitchen floor from being pistol-whipped by Su'.

"Okay, man, I will!" T-Zoe spoke in a deep Haitian accent.

"Let's get out of here," Su'Rabbit said as he vigorously kicked T-Zoe in his temple, knocking him out cold.

Together they tied T-Zoe's hands behind his back with a phone cord and dragged him to the front door. After putting him in the trunk of the Lincoln town car, Johnny and Su'Rabbit successfully torched the place and then made an inconspicuous escape.

* * *

When detectives Harris and Holmes arrived at the Westbrook scene, after leaving the 2nd and 3rd Street scenes, they were exhausted from their vagrant, nimble thoughts of what the hell was going on. One thing they knew for certain was that someone was seriously going at the Haitians, and they had every means of completely destroying them.

"Lisa, all these homes are where suspected drug activities have occurred as reported by the neighbors, who still have claimed to have seen nothing when questioned. Crazy, huh?" Harris realized.

"I was gonna ask you that, Mark. I think it's the birth of a turf war. Like, 'We don't want the Haitians in our hood no more,'" Holmes stated, gesturing quotations with her fingers and explaining her theory as they looked on at the house still ablaze.

They walked together behind the yellow crime scene tape and inspected the six dead Haitian men underneath shrouds laid side by side on the driveway. They were removed from their original spots for safety purposes and away from the fire.

"They're definitely Haitians with these rough features," Holmes exclaimed while looking at the dead Zoes.

"Stuart PD Captain Cummings says the same thing, Lisa," Holmes retorted as he read an incoming text on his iPhone from the captain.

"Are you serious?" Holmes said in disbelief as she the text stood and read on Harris's phone from Cummings, who was at another crime scene in East Stuart.

"Damn! This is real crazy, Mark!" Holmes said, just as a crime scene investigator walked up to her and Harris.

"What's good, Sawyer?" Det. Harris asked the CSI.

He was a young black man in his late twenties, already with the strong potential of becoming a homicide detective.

"Looks like an ambush from the back, cocktails were thrown, and then an exchange of fire. All the victims were nailed, as they had no choice but to run out of the front door."

"Bang! Bang! Bang!" Sawyer said, shooting an invisible gun toward the front door. "Or burn alive!"

"Sounds reasonable, Sawyer," Harris retorted, nodding his head in assent.

"What other possible way?" Sawyer added.

"I gotta admit, you're right, son. I just wish this accuracy could solve the case," Holmes said.

"It's a head start at least," Sawyer suggested.

"Yeah, a son of a bitch head start," Harris said, and then walked off to further investigate the crime at the crack of dawn.

Chapter Thirteen

"Girl, I'm tellin' you, your ass needs to call the man before another bitch grabs him," LeLe told her girl Bellda.

LeLe was also Haitian with a phat ass like Buffy the Body. She and Bellda had niggas on their heels everywhere they went, trying to get their numbers and booty call hour. But they were adamant, taken, and loyal. Though Bellda's patience with Pat had run completely out, it had been weeks since she had sex.

Maybe she's right, Bellda thought while helping LeLe bring in her groceries, along with her bad-ass kids.

"You asked me 'bout him, and I told you, his ex is the bitch, Lala. Her baby daddy just got killed."

"In Indiantown?" Bellda asked curiously.

"Yeah, don't be a fool and let her get what could be yours. The bitch is vulnerable, and they have a past," LeLe said while taking the food from the Publix bags and putting it in the refrigerator.

"How do I know they not creepin'?" Bellda asked.

"They not! That nigga be on the run and 'bout his money ever since T-Gutta been fuckin' with him. T-Gutta been bringing in bankroll," LeLe said.

"Remind me, the nigga put $9,500 on a bitch he don't know from Adam and Eve!"

"A bitch he wants to know. Now call him, girl, and stop playin' bitch!" LeLe persisted.

Darkness had just fallen, and the streets in East Stuart were still shaken by the murders that had occurred the previous night. Since seeing him at the mall and dropping off T-Gutta, he never knew that she was inside the house. Bellda had been thinking about Mr. Handsome like crazy.

"I guess it won't do nothing to call him!" Bellda said.

"Bitch! Call that man!" LeLe exclaimed.

"Alright, damn! How much he payin' you?" Bellda asked.

"Enough to get you off of Pat's sorry ass and get with a nigga who ain't trapped in no relationship," LeLe retorted.

Damn! She's so right! Bellda said as she pulled out her iPhone and dialed Real's number.

* * *

Real was conversing with his cocaine connect that he had finally met up with to get shit popping. His connect was the uncle of an old friend who he had met in prison, who was never hitting the streets again unless he succeeded in an escape.

"So, Chucky tell me that you are good, my friend. He rarely introduces people to his uncle. But when he does, I know that me nephew trusts him," Pablo spoke in his best English.

He was an old-school Mexican, who, unbeknownst to Real, took ownership of 65 percent of the cocaine distribution in Florida. He resided in West Tampa in a luxurious mansion and stayed in Florida only six months of the year. He then went back to Mexico City.

"Chucky is a good friend of mine, Pablo," Real said.

They were dining at the five-star restaurant Capital Grill in Palm Beach Gardens. It was a place no nigga looked fit to be. But Real had come correctly dressed in business attire. He wore a costly cream Polo suit and 14 karat gold rimmed glasses that were not prescription. The twosome ate a delicious, expensive meal and drank the most delicious wine Real had ever tasted.

"Son, listen to me good," Pablo said, holding up his index finger with a serious look on his clean-shaven face.

"One time only, my friend, will I allow you to mess up. You continue to bring me money, my friend, and cop faithfully, and then we'll have no problems. I have a lot of people trying their best to play Pablo's numbers. But without me, no plays at all," Pablo explained to an attentive Real, who had no clue that the same Haitians he was preparing to run off his coast were Pablo's contenders and enemies of one of his client's—Polo.

"A kilo, my friend—28 single, whole, if less than ten. But when you purchase more than ten, we deal faithfully at 17.5 a piece."

Damn! Real thought, bridling his excitement and holding a poker face with Pablo. *Bottle's on me!* Real thought as he felt his iPhone vibrate in his slacks for the umpteenth time within the past hour.

Real assumed that it was a persistent Lala, who he had been avoiding since Joc's murder. He knew he should be consoling her instead of avoiding her, but he had more important matters to take care of, such as taking over the city, buying his kilos for 17.5 a piece, and letting them go under Pat's 25.5 for 20.5 until he had the dope game's attention on their knees.

"Pablo, we will always purchase more than ten," Real informed him.

I know them Haitians ain't copping 17.5 a brick, Real thought.

"Good, my friend. In a few days, I will call you. Whatever you ask for, Pablo will front you on behalf of my nephew

Chucky," Pablo retorted and then clicked champagne glasses with Real. "Welcome to the Mexican Snow Cartel II, my friend. We treat you like family from here out. Any problems you have, we have, and we will clean them up for you."

"Gracias, Pablo!"

"No, gracias, my friend, for lookin' out for me nephew. When the COs sent a man to kill him, you saved me nephew," Pablo said, remembering a time when Real fatally stabbed an assassin in prison who was attempting to stab Chucky from behind in the recreation yard.

Chucky was an M-13 gang member leader who stood five and weighed 185 pounds. He wore a clean bald head and was tatted everywhere. At forty-six years old, Chucky was well respected and known for taking the big dawgs out to stand on top. At the time of Real saving him, they had become good friends.

When Real saw the Mexican CO set the stage for Chucky's assassination, he intercepted the hit and quickly stabbed the assassin six times, instantly killing him. When chaos erupted on the recreation yard, Real moved up on the Mexican CO and stabbed him to death and got away with it as well. Since that chaotic day, Real, Chucky, and Kentucky were brothers with real bonds. Though Chucky slept in a different dorm than the other two, the trio hung out every day in the rec yard.

Feeling his phone vibrate again, Real decided to briefly excuse himself. "Pablo, I'll be a minute, please," Real said as he stood up and then strutted off to the men's restroom.

When he got inside and pulled out his phone, he saw an unknown number.

"Hello," he answered.

"Hi, Real. It's me!" a female voice said that was not Lala yet sounded familiar.

Real just couldn't come straight off his head to place the voice with a face. He was perplexed. "Me who?" Real asked the stranger.

"Damn! You have that many, huh?" she said.

"Man, a nigga ain't got time fo' games. Call me back when you can state yo' name."

"Boy, shut up! This Mookie, and I need to see you when you can."

What the fuck she want? Real thought, more perplexed.

"Is this 'bout Lala?" Real asked.

"No," Mookie said as he got quiet for a moment. Real could hear Keith Sweat playing in the background on low and a soft moan from Mookie. "Lala has nothing to do with this and what I need from you tonight," she retorted seductively.

"Is that right?" Real asked, catching the drift.

"Yes, Real. It's been right since our first kiss."

Mookie reminded Real of their childhood crush that didn't go past a kiss in middle school. When he had gotten with Lala, no woman was able to break his attention from her. She had him hooked and deeply in love.

"Where you at?" Real asked.

"I'm in Palm Beach at the Holiday Inn. Room 302. I just came here to get some me time, and I just couldn't get you off my mind. I'm not looking for no obligations. Just one night, Real," she said in a low purr while playing with her phat pussy.

"That shit wet?" Real asked as his dick became erect.

"Yes, Real. It's so wet, tight, phat. Please come. Ummm! Real, I'm coming, uhhh!" Mookie moaned out as she came to an orgasm.

"Holiday Inn on Military," Real asked.

"Yes!" Mookie moaned.

"I'll be there in an hour," Real said as he hung up. "I been wanting that chocolate bitch for a long time," Real stated while looking at another unknown number on his phone.

Who the hell is this? he thought.

But he decided to hit the number in the morning when he was done with Ms. Gorgeous Mookie. For all he knew, the whole Ms. Gorgeous clique wanted to fuck.

If so, I sho' ain't 'bout to spare shit just 'cause of Lala, Real thought as he returned to Pablo to conduct further business.

* * *

Lala was exhausted at waiting up for Real to come in. She showered and got changed into her sexy pajamas. She then sat in the living room with her sleeping two-year-old baby girl, who would never know her father other than seeing his life in pictures. Joc's death pained her deeply, and she cried her well dry from grieving.

For a couple days now, Lala had distanced herself from everyone, even her clique of Ms. Gorgeouses, while handling funeral arrangements for Joc. But now she needed comfort, and she only wanted comfort and love from Real. She wiped her eyes, catching her tears while rubbing her daughter's back, who was comfortably asleep on the sofa. Looking at the picture of Joc and her daughter, Destiny, on her iPhone, Lala broke down into hysterics. She tried calling up Real again, but once again it was to no avail.

"Please, Real, come home!" she softly cried.

* * *

Real was in paradise with Mookie and was loving every moment of sexing her. The bitch had all types of tricks up her sleeves, and she made sure she outdid Lala's performance. At the crack of dawn, Mookie was sucking on Real's dick as a good morning greeting. She was a superb dick sucker and knew how to make a nigga's head spin, toes curl, and ass cheeks lock up.

Damn! Real thought, watching her swallow his length while slightly gagging.

"Umm!" she moaned as she slowly sucked Real's dick.

When she came up, she made a loud wet popping sound with her mouth as she pulled his dick out while beginning to stroke him.

"All these years and this is what you've been missin'. You knew Lala couldn't fuck with me, especially a bad bitch like me. But you still overlooked me!" Mookie exclaimed as she climbed on top of Real and slowly descended down his rock-hard dick.

"Don't worry 'bout the past. Let's focus on now and enjoy every moment unregretfully," Real retorted.

"Trust me, Real. I don't regret, ummm, nothing about, ummm, us. Just fuck me and appreciate me!" Mookie purred as she sped up her pace while riding his dick.

"I will," Real promised while he watched her chocolate titties bounce as she rapidly rode his dick.

* * *

Pat was furious about what was occurring in Martin County, and so was Black. The moment that Black had discovered the devastating news from Pat, an emergency meeting between the two was summoned.

"Pat, I want Shamoney brought to me alive."

"I seriously don't think he's behind it."

"Pat, stop being stupid, son!" Black exploded.

He's possessed. He doesn't see the face of the enemy, Black thought.

"Martin County is the gold mine. It has made us millions, Pat, and someone is clearly saying 'get the fuck out of my town' by killing our men. Polo is not the man claiming the wrath; however, he is another problem, Pat!" Black angrily spat in Creole.

"Find T-Zoe, B-Zoe, and whoever it's gonna take to bring Shamoney to me, and watch how I break his ass!" Black retorted.

I knew we made a mistake cuttin' off Shamoney! Pat badly wanted to tell his superior but thought otherwise.

"I got you, Haitian," he replied instead.

* * *

Whip!

"Please! No more! I tell the truth!" T-Zoe shouted in devastating pain after being struck with a horse whip by Su'Rabbit.

Su'Rabbit had brought T-Zoe to an old warehouse he owned that was deep in the woods in Hobe Sound, another section of Martin County along Bridge Road. They were deep out west where no one could hear a sound. Su' inherited the land from his great-grandfather Buck, who once ran a farm on the patch of land. It was Su'Rabbit's land to do with as he pleased. He chose to utilize it as a human butcher shop. T-Zoe had been beaten to a bloody mess with horse whips by Su' and Johnny. He literally looked like a tiger had gotten a hold of him.

T-Zoe hung from the warehouse joist a foot off the ground from his wrists that were bound by a rope. He was talking and giving Su'Rabbit, Johnny, Real, and Shamoney the entire scope of the inside of the Haitian mafia. To Shamoney's surprise a lot had changed since the first man had been lost. Real knew that he had to go after Pat to get to Black, something that Shamoney persisted telling him would be formidable.

Nothing in my plans to take over was planned to be easy, Real thought as he watched Su'Rabbit and Johnny continue to beat T-Zoe.

Real was sure that T-Zoe had given up everything.

Whip!

"Awww! Man, that's it! Please! Please stop!" T-Zoe begged not to be struck again with the whip.

"Su'! Hold on a minute!" Real halted him as he walked up to a bloody and naked T-Zoe. "Where do I find Black?" Real asked a wincing T-Zoe.

"Miami!" he could barely get out.

"So, B-Zoe killed my niggas, and he lives in Ft. Pierce, you say?" Real inquired.

For the umpteenth time, T-Zoe voraciously replied, "Yes. He was paid a lot by Pat!"

Real turned around and looked at his brother Shamoney.

"We go after Pat now. I thought I'd enjoy seeing him defend his establishment. But I've had a change of heart, and I want to see B-Zoe myself," Real said before a brief pause. "Su'Rabbit," Real spoke.

"What's up, homie?" Su' responded.

"Feed this nigga to the gators," Real ordered as he stormed off with Shamoney on his heels.

"I got ya, my nigga," Su'Rabbit exclaimed as T-Zoe mumbled something indiscernible in Creole.

"What was that T-Zoe?" Johnny asked him, who again mumbled in Creole.

An hour later, Su'Rabbit and Johnny had driven to Ft. Pierce (Killa County)—to the infamous Taylor Creek where thousands of souls had been taken—and fed T-Zoe to three adult hungry alligators, alive.

The gators tore his body into fractions, completely erasing him from the face of the earth.

"Now that's how a swamp boy gets off!" Johnny exclaimed.

"Swamp boy get off!" Su'Rabbit shouted, reciting the lyrics to his cousin Thead's hit single that went gold and got him signed with Slip-n-Slide Records.

Chapter Fourteen

When Real awoke from a power nap, which he only intended to last a couple hours, he heard his iPhone ringing on the nightstand. Stretching his eyes while simultaneously grabbing the phone, he then glided his thumb across the flat screen and answered the call. "Hello," he said, slumberous.

"Why is it so hard to catch up wit' you? I'm saying, you give me yo' number, and you don't even pick up," a sexy female voice with an accent fired back seductively.

Real sat straight up in bed, deeply perplexed as to whom the voice belonged. When he checked the number, he saw that it was the missed unknown call to whom he had forgotten to call back.

"Who this?" Real asked.

"This is the bitch you put $9,500 on a necklace who you didn't know from Adam and Eve!"

"Bellda!" Real threw out her name.

"Nah, Bellda," she sassily retorted.

"Now you want to call a nigga. It shows me how much you really appreciate a nigga. What's up?" Real retorted, intending to get under her skin and make her feel bad.

When he heard her suck her teeth, he knew he had Bellda right where he wanted her.

"Sorry, even though I don't know why I'm sayin' it, but I did appreciate it. Matter of fact, I have it on now. And I think I found a nice dress to wear with it," Bellda added.

"Oh yeah? Where are, you going in the dress?" Real asked.

"Wherever you plan on taking a real woman. I hope you have good taste," Bellda playfully insulted Real.

"You have a mouth like Ali's daughter. I wonder if you can back it up like her," Real added.

"Nigga! I almost told you something," Bellda said as she again sucked her teeth.

"And what is that?" Real inquired.

"How 'bout you come to Salerno to 2032 Innez Street around 8:00 p.m. and see," she said.

"2032?" Real repeated.

"Yeah, I'll text it to you when I hang up," Bellda promised.

"Do that!" Real retorted the moment Lala entered the room with Destiny in her arms.

What the fuck! How did she get in here? Real wanted to know.

"Get yourself together. I'll be waiting, handsome," Bellda said before she hung up.

When she was gone, Real looked at Lala sourly.

"How did you get in, Lala?" Real asked, bridling his temper.

"What do you mean, Real? Am I not supposed to be around you since Joc's—" she paused short of what she wanted to say, on the verge of tears.

Real clearly saw her pain. She was a mess.

"Since Joc died, you've been avoiding me, Real. What's wrong?" Lala asked, throwing her daughter on her left hip.

"Lala, listen. I don't want you gettin' shit twisted. We are not and never will get back on the level of a relationship, and you know why. We cool friends, but right now—"

"No!" Lala whispered as she began to slowly break down, shaking her head from side to side.

"And we are not going to be kicking it sexually anymore."

116

"Oh, so you done found somebody? Now it's 'fuck Lala,' huh?" she screamed with tears cascading down her face.

Little Destiny began to cry, sensing her mother's discomfort.

"Stop it, Destiny!" Lala exploded, violently shaking her daughter in the air. "Shut up!"

Real quickly leaped from the bed and grabbed Destiny out of Lala's hands.

Smack!

He then vigorously slapped Lala's ass to the ground.

"What the fuck is wrong with you, huh?" Real exploded, holding on to Destiny while looking at Lala hysterically crying on the ground.

He didn't care whose child it was. Child abuse did not sit well with him, and he did not regret putting his hands on Lala.

"Real, I'm so sorry, baby! Sorry!" Lala cried out as Destiny instantly calmed down in Real's arms, lying her head on his shoulder.

"Lala, get out of my shit and leave the key! Don't ever let me see you treat yo' daughter like that because of your frustration—of a man. Take that shit out on me. Do you hear me?" Real spoke sternly.

Lala nodded her head up and down in assent.

"Yes, Real. I hear you."

Real sat Destiny on the bed and then stormed back into the bathroom, locking the door behind him.

"Get out, Lala, and leave my key on the table!" he shouted over the running shower water.

Lala couldn't believe that Real was ending it with her. But she wouldn't allow herself to continue to cry over spilled milk. She would wait until she saw who the bitch was for whom he was booting her out of his life. Until then, she had a baby daddy to bury in two days.

Real, I'll show you how to cut a bitch off. I made a mistake by leaving you, I know. But I will not make the mistake of losing you. First love will also be home! she pondered as she left Real's apartment with Destiny in her arms, leaving her spare key on the table like he had demanded.

* * *

When Chantele saw her husband sitting in the waiting lobby at Palm Beach Airport engrossed in his iPhone, she instantly realized how much she had missed him. As she tried creeping up on him from behind, he surprised her by turning around and shooting an air gun at her with his hand.

Pow! Pow! Pow!

"I been seeing you, baby girl. Busted!" Shamoney exclaimed as he stood up to hug his baby, who was killing every bitch in the vicinity.

A few folks had recognized her as a swimsuit model and asked for her autograph. Generously, she gave a few of them her autograph and then gleefully walked away with her husband.

"Damn, celebrity!" Shamoney said when they were in the Maybach that Pat had given him as a going-away gift.

"Whatever, bae. You act like you not likin' the package of havin' a celebrity as a wife. If you've been listening, I'm the swimsuit cover girl, baby."

"Get the fuck out of here!" Shamoney exclaimed to his wife.

Truth be told, his mind was so engrossed on the streets, that he hadn't been paying attention to anything in the media, other than the news that he and his brother were creating.

"So, when are the funerals?" Chantele asked.

It was her only reason of coming home on an emergency call to support her husband at his homeboys' funerals.

"Two days. Until then, we're going to be locked away in our room. Just the two of us!" Shamoney said as he reached over to kiss his wife on the lips.

"Oh, is that right?" Chantele asked seductively.

"Yo name is Mrs. Wilkins, right?" he asked his wife while licking his lips and looking over at his sexy, caramel wife who stood five two.

He was unaware of the increase in the size of her nose and weight.

He has no clue! Chantele thought as she replied to his question.

"Yes, it is, and I wear it proudly, daddy."

"I know, baby," Shamoney said as he pecked her on the lips again and then burned rubber as he exited the airport.

"Boy, slow down before we get a damn ticket!" Chantele exclaimed in laughter.

"Fuck the police and their tickets. They got to catch us first, baby!" he shouted as he turned up the volume to Boosie's hit "Wipe Me Down."

* * *

When Bellda stepped out the door in a lustrous skin-tight, black spaghetti-strap dress and some leopard Dolce Vita heels, wearing the *XO* necklace around her neck, Real almost lost his manners, gawking at her undulations with lust-filled eyes. He was a gentleman who opened the passenger door for her to his new BMW SUV. On the seat, Bellda found a dozen red roses and smiled brightly.

"For me?"

"For you!" Real retorted to a blushing Bellda, who grabbed the roses, smelled them, and then hopped inside.

"Thanks, Jermaine," she expressed her gratification.

"You look gorgeous, baby gal," Real complimented while licking his lips and hanging into the passenger door.

Bellda began blushing to the extreme as she absentmindedly grabbed hold of Real's tie and pulled him into her. She then gave him a soft peck on his lips.

"Be good. I'm overdue, so please don't spoil it. Because there's more where that kiss just came from," Bellda warned him, with a sexy Haitian accent.

"Never that, beautiful," Real said as he closed her door.

As he walked around to the driver's seat, she could still smell his Polo cologne.

Damn! This nigga got it going' on fo' real! she thought, admiring Real in his fresh-ass ocean blue Armani tailor-made suit.

When Real got inside, he turned the blasting AC down low and put on some Tyrese Gibson. Bellda was already giving him a ten, because unbeknownst to him, she was fucked up about Tyrese.

"I love his music," Bellda informed Real.

"Is that a good sign?" Real said while pulling his goatee. "Or do I need to beat up Tyrese's ass, huh?"

His comment got a laugh out of her.

"Is that a way of sayin' you throwing the cuffs on me?" Bellda frankly asked.

Real looked Bellda in her adorable eyes and smiled, showing his gleaming gold teeth.

"It's in my considerations," Real retorted.

A long forty-five minutes later, Real pulled up to Capital Grill, which Bellda knew was expensive.

What nigga spends $200 a plate? Bellda thought.

"You know of this place?" Real asked as he pulled up to the entrance.

"Yeah, this is a very nice and expensive-ass place," she said as the six foot two, skinny white valet opened her door and assisted her out with a gentle hand.

"Take care of the car. One scratch, and it's me and you," Real warned the other tall valet, to whom Real gave his keys when he walked around to meet up with Bellda.

She's never been catered to like this, Real concluded after espying the nervous look in her eyes.

"It's okay, baby! We cool, right?" Real asked as he offered his arm for Bellda to intertwine.

"Yes, Jermaine. We are cool," she replied with her sexy-ass Haitian accent that made his head spin every time she talked.

When the duo stepped inside, she was surprised to see that reservations had already been made. On the other hand, Real was surprised to see that they weren't the only black couple in the pricey restaurant. Bellda's ass jiggled lustrously with every step she took in her skin-tight dress that accentuated her voluptuous body. Real knew without a doubt that he had stepped into the building with a bad-ass bitch, just by looking at all the men who, despite sitting with their dates, still cut their eyes at Bellda's undulations.

* * *

Despite the block being hot with roaming unmarked police cars, V-Money was still making a killing serving the fiends and setting up shop with the help of a couple young niggas.

Jake's store was back as usual, with the guys playing craps and poker on the side of the building. Every hustler was chasing down the fiends with competitive-sized crack cocaine rocks. But it wasn't the same to everyone not to hear Joc's loud, obnoxious mouth when he was gambling. It was understood more than unspoken. Meat Head was a quiet man, and he was being missed as well.

When Pimp pulled up to Jake's store in her watermelon box Chevy Caprice on twenty-eight-inch rims, bumping to Old Master P's "I Miss My Homies," a lot of niggas got in their feelings and turned Jake's store into yet another vigil for Joc and Meat Head. They bought out Jake's cheap candles and lit them while sipping on liquor and orange juice.

Damn! I miss my niggas! V-Money thought, catching the tears that fell from his eyes.

"It's okay, V-Money. He was all our homie," Pimp said to him as she hugged him and cried with him in his arms.

Together, they consoled each other endearingly, letting their grief transparently accentuate their affection for each other.

* * *

After leaving Capital Grill, Real took Bellda on a romantic stroll along the beautiful beach in Palm Beach, until he found a nice spot to lay down the comfy blanket that he had brought along with him. For hours, they had been staring at the water under a full moon and sky full of stars light-years away.

Bellda's feet sat in Real's lap while he massaged them affectionately. She was extremely moved by his delicate touch and wanted him to explore her entire body with the same hands. The wine in her system from dinner had her attentive to every touch as he caressed her delicate feet. They knew a lot about each other in just one night and felt like they had known each other their whole lives.

Real was honest with her about his prison bid, and he trusted her to know about his street life and what he did for a living. She knew everything except him being the ringleader of the headline murders of her Haitian kin. And she had informed him on everything about her love life in the past and of the many times she had been hurt. But she did leave out the part about the man who she was definitely leaving for Real.

Pat is definitely out of the picture. Money is not always the winner, Bellda thought as she was engrossed in the contentedness that Real was fulfilling that night.

"What's roaming through yo' head that got you all quiet?" Real asked, snapping Bellda from her daydreaming state.

She looked at him and seriously contemplated what she was about to commit herself to. She didn't want to come off with the wrong impression on the first night.

But damn, this nigga is dead handsome! she thought.

"Can I be honest with you?" Bellda asked, pulling her feet back and then sitting Indian style.

"Sure you can. It's the best—"

Before Real could finish his sententious saying, Bellda was all over him. She roughly and deeply kissed him while popping the buttons on his Polo dress shirt. As she climbed into his lap, she began to unfasten his Polo belt with ease. She lay back with Real while straddling him and still kissing him.

Real wasted no time sliding his hands up her dress, feeling her succulent and pantiless ass. When he swiped his fingers across her wet mouth and fondled her sensitive throbbing clitoris, Bellda let out a loud moan. Real took charge as he flipped her onto her back while he simultaneously pulled down his slacks and briefs. He slid Bellda's dress over her hips and teased her by placing the head of his throbbing dick on her throbbing clitoris.

"This what you want, ma?" Real asked for further consent.

No words needed to be uttered for Bellda, as she extended her legs and artistically wrapped her stallion thighs around Real's waist, bringing him down into her as he plunged deeply inside her wet, phat, tight pussy.

"Uhhh shit!" she exhaled, gaping until she found his neck, onto which she gently bit down.

Damn! This pussy already got me fucked up, Real thought as he penetrated Bellda long, hard, and passionately.

When they came, the duo came together, and like Bellda had warned Real, she was overdue and backed up as she came convulsively to an electrifying orgasm.

Chapter Fifteen

The enormous antique St. John Baptist Church in East Stuart was overcrowded with friends and family attending both Joc's and Meat Head's funerals, which were being held together. The entire swamp was there showing their respects, as were others who knew both friends throughout the entire Treasure Coast.

Reverend Weaver from Hobe Sound directed the funeral, and touched a lot of souls in the church. Real sat in the sixth row with Shamoney and Chantele, who were dressed like twins in all-black attire. Real kept a close eye on Lala, who sat with Joc's mother and family. Behind her were all the Ms. Gorgeouses, constantly crying for the bodies that lay in the black closed caskets front and center in the church. What Reverend Weaver was preaching on reminded Real exactly why he had to go hard or else not even play the game.

"People, we only have one precious life to live, and a more precious life to live when death comes in either odds or evens," Reverend Weaver spoke as the organ sounded. "We not cryin' 'cause of death," he said as he wiped away the sweat from his face with a rag. "We cryin' for joy!"

The organ chimed again.

"Peace! Freedom! Bliss!"

"Amen!" an elderly woman stood with joy, causing more in attendance to stand up in spiritual ovation.

"Hallelujah! Yes, Lord!" Reverend Weaver exclaimed while jumping up and down. "We not crying for sadness. God is here today! He has called these men home. Amen! And we gon' celebrate, Lord! Hallelujah!" the reverend preached hysterically as the organ sounded and sent the Holy Ghost through the church.

When Real looked over at Lala, he saw her breaking down. He then made eye contact with Mookie, who was consoling Lala with Pimp, Nut-Nut, and Luscious. When Real looked to his right, he saw Var being consoled by Alleycat and V-Money.

Damn, my two niggas gone fo' real! he thought as the reality finally dawned on him; and like everyone else who tried to bridle their emotions but failed, he cried too.

But he cried with blood in his eyes for B-Zoe, and retaliation for his homies nowhere near finished in his heart. Real stood up and excused himself. He had to get outside to catch some fresh air.

"Brah, if you want, we can go outside," Real whispered into Shamoney's ear, who nodded his head, grabbed Chantele's hand, and proceeded out the door.

They found T-Gutta outside the church as well, getting some air and smoking a phat kush blunt.

"You too, huh?" Real asked him.

"It's too much. Funerals and me never get along. I don't even want to attend my own!" T-Gutta retorted as he passed over the blunt to Real while looking at Shamoney and his wife hold each other. "Brah got a bad one," T-Gutta complimented Shamoney's wife to Real.

"Yeah, he did that!" Real added.

The music in the church could be heard from outside. As Real looked up at the overcast sky, a sound of thunder exploded, causing him to smile. "You know what that means, T-Gutta!"

"Hell yeah, brah! It means our niggas are in heaven today," T-Gutta said.

"That's right, my nigga," Real assented.

* * *

When Big Chub, Pat, and the rest of the entourage pulled up to the luxurious palace in Port St. Lucie, Pat saw that the Maybach he had given Shamoney was sitting in the driveway along with his .745. There were six men in the two SUVs, and every man was carrying M-16 rifles. They all exited the SUVs together and approached the front door.

On the side of the palace in an access driveway that led to the backyard, Pat saw a parked cleaning service.

"We got some company," Pat told everyone as he artistically and successfully picked the lock to the front door.

Once inside the house, the cleaning service crew of illegal immigrants was caught off guard attending to the opulent home. The frightened men and women were all immediately gunned down by Pat's men.

"Strip this bitch down!" Pat ordered his men to ransack Shamoney and Chantele's precious home.

* * *

The block in East Stuart was jumping with the new product that Real had put out, and the fiends were going crazy. It was heaven for the dope boys, who saw the dramatic increase in money. The kilos were going for 20.5, and the ounces were 5.75 a piece. With the Haitians out of the area, it was all game. Real and Shamoney were making a killing shutting shit down.

The gambling house on Tarpon was loud and raucous as usual, with young niggas shooting dice and playing poker. Everyone inside the house hit the deck when the rapid shots exploded outside.

"Oh shit!" a couple niggas howled.

Some niggas weren't as fortunate and got hit with stray bullets that came crashing through the windows.

"Damn!" a young nigga named Quinton shouted while immersing low, cocking back his Glock .40, and running out the front door and squeezing at the fleeing SUV.

Boom! Boom! Boom!

When Quinton's Glock jammed, he found himself in trouble, but it was too late to retreat.

Chop! Chop! Chop! Chop!

The AK-47 bullets from the SUV riddled his body like swiss cheese, letting off a full thirty-clip into the young man.

As the heavy rain fell from the sky and washed away Quinton's blood, all that was left of him was the blank stare in his eyes. The lifeless twenty-one-year-old Quinton was slumped against the bullet-riddled bubble Caprice Chevy on twenty-eight-inch rims.

* * *

When B-Zoe made it to the Ramada Inn in Stuart, he and his two soldiers abandoned the stolen SUV and then hopped into another legit SUV.

"Man, I can't believe that lil nigga tried some Rambo shit!" B-Zoe said, speaking of the young man he had just taken out with his AK-47 in East Stuart.

"That lil nigga thought shit was sweet!" B-Zoe's soldier David retorted while sparking flame to a phat dro blunt and passing it to B-Zoe, who was driving.

"A lot of niggas 'bout to fall fo' my nigga T-Zoe," another soldier, Skinny Zoe, said from the backseat.

"This shit just getting started," B-Zoe exclaimed.

He was missing his nigga T-Zoe. B-Zoe knew that T-Zoe was dead somewhere, and he just wanted to make sure that his nigga had a proper burial.

B-Zoe wasn't naive, and he refused to be in the statistics of it. He knew well that niggas who died in the streets sometimes went missing and were never found. But he would never guess or expect for T-Zoe's remains to be in the bellies of three alligators in the infamous Taylor Creek.

* * *

The news about the fatal drive-by shooting that had occurred on Tarpon Street quickly circulated and got back to Real and Shamoney, along with everyone else, at the cemetery in Port Mayaca. It was the grave site fifteen miles outside of Indiantown where every dead soldier from the swamp was buried. The heavy downpour made many scramble, mainly those who lacked an umbrella.

The rain is strong symbolic assurance that both homies are in heaven, Real and others considered.

Real, T-Gutta, Lunatic, and Var all came to the grave site, while Shamoney and Chantele went home to ready themselves for the after party at a reception center in the swamp,

"What's good, brah?" Real asked T-Gutta, who'd had a bothered look on his face since he heard about the shooting in his hood.

"I gotta find out who did that shit. It's like we lose a nigga every other day, dirty," T-Gutta explained while watching the dirt get poured onto Joc's and Meat Head's caskets.

The stage was too much for Lala and her clique, who had left with the rest of the crowd after Reverend Weaver's last prayer for the departed men.

"Don't worry, brah," Real said as he rubbed the fatigue from his face with his hands. "From here on out, I don't care what hood a nigga from. He from Martin and he drop, then we dropping three of theirs. We know who's responsible," Real declared among his circle.

T-Gutta had lost his childhood homie Mike James that day. He was a go-getter and stupid-ass nigga who said anything out of his mouth to anybody.

"Even if we gotta go get 'em out of the city, we goin', nigga," Real added as he felt the vibration of his iPhone in his slacks. When he retrieved his phone and saw it was Shamoney, he quickly answered. "What's up, my nigga?" he inquired.

He could hear crying in the background, and instantly he knew it was Chantele.

Something's wrong, Real thought, sensing something amiss.

He heard Shamoney release a sigh and then begin to speak angrily, "All my cleaning service people are dead, and my home is destroyed." He paused and then sighed again. "The house is a wreck, and I know it's Pat."

"Don't go nowhere, brah. He trying to lure you into a trap. He knows that out of all people, you'll suspect him first. We goin' to get him together, lil brah!" Real insisted to a dead line.

Shamoney was gone.

"Hello!" Real called out into the phone again. "Damn it!" Real exploded, knowing his brother wasn't hearing anything he had to say.

Real knew how much of a hot-head Shamoney could be, and when blood was in his eyes, he only saw one thing: the objective.

"What's good, brah?" T-Gutta asked with concern.

"Shamoney's crib got hit, and he 'bout to go at this nigga himself. It's a trap, and he 'bout to walk right into it!" Real exclaimed as he made a dash from underneath the tent and out into the rain along with T-Gutta, Var, and Lunatic on his heels.

Real jumped into his SUV with T-Gutta while Var and Lunatic hopped into Lunatic's Dodge Durango. Together the foursome burned rubber leaving the grave site.

Little brother, don't fall for the bait! Real thought, pushing ninety miles per hour on Highway 76/Kanner.

"Damn it!" Real exclaimed, hammering the steering wheel. "T-Gutta, call Shamoney. He's not pickin' up for me. He knows I'ma talk him out of goin' by himself," Real said while trying to hit up Johnny but to no avail.

Johnny was the only person who was missing from the funeral. He just didn't do funerals, and neither did his ace, Su'Rabbit.

"Shit!" Real exclaimed.

"He not pickin' up, brah," T-Gutta said as he was also ignored by Shamoney.

"Stubborn bitch!" Real exploded, increasing the speed to the max of 125 mph on Highway 76, in hopes of catching his brother and saving his life.

He had no clue where Pat lived in Palm Beach County. Real just knew that he had to get to St. Lucie County to prepare for the worst or best of his brother's stupid decision to war on his own.

Chapter Sixteen

After getting off the phone with Real, Shamoney had quickly gathered the money from the attic safe above the guest room, which the invaders had missed. Shamoney knew exactly who he was going after, and despite Chantele's pleas to leave it alone and call the police, he was determined and his mind was already made up.

"Baby, please just let the police—"

"Chantele, listen to me. The police are only concerned 'bout one thing, and that's to lock up my ass. I'ma be okay," Shamoney said to her as they pulled up to the West Palm Beach Airport, where Chantele was scheduled to catch a flight back to New York City.

Shamoney stepped out of the car and walked around to open Chantele's door. All she could think about was his safety, and she didn't want to leave his side. As much as she didn't want to deal with him and his street life anymore, she was considering a divorce until she discovered that she was pregnant with his child.

I can't let him do this! she thought as Shamoney opened her door.

"Come on, baby. I gotta get you out of here," Shamoney said.

He knew that shit was about to get real, and like any king in war, he had to protect this queen.

Getting her away from the predestined chaos was his only concern at the moment. When Chantele looked up with a flood of tears cascading down her face, Shamoney's heart fell to his gut to see her in such pain, which deeply hurt him.

"I love you, Shada," Chantele spoke, calling him by his first name. "I don't want to lose you, but if this is our last time, just know that me and your child will miss you," she broke down.

Child! Shamoney thought, realizing what his wife was concisely telling him.

Shamoney then pulled her from the car to her feet and held her in his arms.

"Baby, daddy gon' be straight. I don't need you to stress, okay?" Shamoney said, rubbing Chantele's curly locks. "I know how much you want me to get out of these streets," he said as he pulled her back to look into her eyes. "I promise, when I handle these niggas, we gon' be out of this shit together. Don't worry 'bout what you saw at the house. I will handle it."

"What do you mean, Shada? Them people we hired have family."

"Them under the table, and nine out of ten are illegal immigrants," he explained.

"Shada, I'm pregnant. Didn't you hear me?" Chantele exploded, hitting Shamoney on his chest.

Shamoney grabbed Chantele and held her tightly.

"Baby, I'm gonna be okay. Please trust me, okay?" Shamoney asked of his wife.

She bridled her emotions and let his words comfort her.

There's nothing I can do. His mind is determined! she thought as she planted her lips to his and kissed him long and passionately.

Shamoney tasted the salty tears that fell from her eyes on her lips. He had to make it back to her and not leave her or his child alone to fight the world. Despite her lifestyle, Chantele loved Shamoney and found herself trapped in his world.

"I love you, Shada. Be careful, will you?"

"I will, baby. And I'll call you in the morning," he informed her.

Together they walked into the airport to book her flight. Neither of them was aware of the eyes watching them from the black SUV.

* * *

If anyone knew the streets of Palm Beach County, Shamoney felt that it was him, being that he had a strong clientele base within the city of Murderville. He had made out the SUV a couple of lights ago, and now he was planning on how he was going to paint their world red, which further prompted him to go after Pat by himself. His anger impaired his ability to make logical decisions, and he was more than thankful for the niggas trailing him, because he was on his way to Lake Worth headfirst.

I'm about to give y'all niggas some real gratification! Shamoney thought as he came to a red light at the intersection of Military and North Lake.

His fully loaded MAC-10 sat on his lap as he closely watched the SUV. They were playing him two cars back.

Shamoney's iPhone chimed in with Yo Gotti's hit "Down in the DM" ringtone. When he looked at the caller, he saw that it was his brother Real again, who had been persistently calling him since he had hung up on him. Shamoney again ignored his brother's call and pressed on the gas while gearing though the green light. Like he expected, when he changed lanes, the SUV did as well.

"Come on, muthafucka!" Shamoney exclaimed over Future's hit emanating from his stereo system at mid volume.

When Shamoney came to the intersection of Okeechobee Boulevard, he abruptly maneuvered to the far-left lane while simultaneously completely dropping down his window. Horns blared from angry drivers, and the niggas in the SUV became perplexed. They were now four cars behind in the same lane as Shamoney, who was two cars behind the first U-turn. With his MAC-10 in his hand and moving in first gear, Shamoney prepared himself for whatever was to come his way.

When it was his turn to hit the U-turn, he did so artistically while aiming at the SUV and releasing a deadly, shocking fusillade at its windshield and hitting both men. The SUV crashed into the car in front of it while they tried to escape the gunfire, but to no avail. Both men in the SUV felt the wrath of the MAC-10.

Shamoney abruptly stopped and hopped out of his car with his MAC-10, simultaneously spraying the SUV with slugs. He ran up to the back door and saw no one in the backseat, which was clearly visible from the shattered windows. He then aimed at both men's heads in the driver and passenger seats and finished them off by exploding their heads with the rapid slugs.

"Tell Pat 'let's run this shit!'" Shamoney said as he made a dash for his .745.

Shamoney then swiftly geared the .745, circling the intersection by taking a back street. He then took Okeechobee Boulevard to Bee Line Highway, where he accelerated to the swamp.

* * *

When Pat's iPhone rang, he saw that it was Shamoney. He was sitting in his den with Big Chub awaiting a call from two of his entourage to inform him that they had Shamoney. Pat was perplexed while staring at Shamoney's name lighting up his phone.

"They must have him and they're calling from his phone!" Pat assumed.

Big Chub was smashing a plate of Gina's delicious barbecue ribs, chicken, and yellow rice.

"Why call from his phone?" Big Chub asked while licking the sauce from his fat fingers.

"I don't know," Pat responded as he answered the phone. "Speak!" Pat barked, getting an ear full of Shamoney laughing hysterically.

"What, Pat? You thought that a nigga would fall for the bait, huh?" Shamoney shrilled.

Pat immediately put the call on speaker so Big Chub could hear.

"What the fuck you talkin' 'bout, nigga?" Pat asked while checking the blinds to his den.

"Pat, two niggas equals two bodies when you send them at me. I thought you were smarter than that, Pat."

Shit! Pat thought.

He couldn't say that he was surprised that Shamoney had taken out his two good men, because he knew who he was dealing with when it came to him on the other side. *A stupid nigga whose finger always stays on the trigger, ready to go!* Pat thought.

"Since you think I'm stupid enough to come to yo' home, how 'bout I show you a trick or two. Take a wild guess what my next move is, Pat," Shamoney said before he hung up.

"Shit!" Pat yelled.

He didn't need to think twice about his two men. He knew that neither of them had an inch of breath left in their bodies.

If I had just talked with Shamoney. Damn, man! Pat thought.

"Chub, we gotta get this lil nigga, and we can't underestimate him," Pat explained.

"Yeah, I know," Chub retorted.

Chapter Seventeen

Six Months Later

The death toll from Martin County to St. Lucie County had increased dramatically. There were murders ever night and day between the Martin County niggas and the Haitians in Killa County. The Haitians within Ft. Pierce were at odds, because not only did they have to worry about Real and Shamoney's force in Martin, but from certain hoods in Ft. Pierce who had mad love for Chyna Man—Johnny.

As the beef cooked up, Black and Pat were both bothered and nervous as hell. Not only were they watching Real and Shamoney take over the streets, but they were also running from Polo's wrath, which had forced Black out of Miami Gardens in an attempt to capture him. All of Pat's entourage was killed by Polo except for Big Chub, who had managed to escape the deadly raid when Zo'pound ambushed the entourage at a club in Miami. Pat was also forced to relocate for the benefit of his family's safety. He was afraid that Shamoney would appear one day with his death sentence, so he moved Gina and his kids into another gorgeous baby mansion further west in Naples.

On the other hand, Shamoney had put up his mansion for $1.5 million, more than what they had paid for it, and sold it in two weeks. They now lived in an even more beautiful mansion on Hutchinson Island in Stuart in Martin County. Down the street from his home, Real and Bellda had their own palace and had become a solid couple in a committed relationship. Real still had no knowledge of Bellda's relationship with Pat, who she had abruptly stopped seeing and ignored all calls from. She decided to put her focus completely on the man who kept a genuine smile upon her face. Her girl LeLe stayed at her and Real's place like it was her own.

Lying in bed at the crack of dawn, Bellda emerged from bed, barefoot and nude. She slid into a satin robe and smiled, as she was engulfed in complete gratification and bliss.

In just six months, this nigga has taken over the city and claimed his queen, she thought as she stared at a sleeping Real in their king-sized bed with a plush canopy, silk sheets, and see-through drapes.

I can live like this forever, Bellda thought, tempted to wake Real with her superb head game.

She half-bridled a chuckle when she thought of a conversation she and LeLe had recently had: "Girl, if I was you, I'd keep that nigga's dick in my mouth. Look how these niggas bow down to him. Shit! He and his brother are gods. And the baby one. What's his name?"

"Johnny," Bellda answered.

"Yeah, he's just as bad as them. Thank God that T-Gutta is one of their disciples," LeLe exclaimed.

That girl is a mess, Bellda thought as she walked into the unique, spacious kitchen to fix her man a delicious breakfast before she was off to work.

Despite her man's accessible six figures and desire for her to quit her job, Bellda remained steadfast and continued to work at the nursing home in Port St. Lucie. She had bonded with her elderly patients, and compassionately cared for them. She had worked drudgingly to obtain her CNA license and was still striving to become an RN. Real complemented her daily on her ambition and thoroughly supported her in whatever needs and wants that she had.

Bellda stood with her hands on her hips in the middle of the kitchen as she contemplated what she was going to make Real for breakfast.

"I think bacon, fried eggs, sausage, grits, and some buttered toast would suit him well," Bellda said to herself.

Maybe LeLe can help me come up with something, and I'll stop by and give her a plate on my way to work, Bellda thought as she went back into the bedroom to grab her phone.

She saw that Real had stirred in his sleep and had shifted from lying on his back to his side. She quietly grabbed her phone from the nightstand on her side of the bed and walked back into the kitchen to call LeLe. When she booted up her phone, there were innumerable and persistent calls from Pat, like always.

Can't this nigga get the picture? Bellda thought angrily as she deleted all of his calls. *This nigga gonna make me change my number, because one day Real's gonna catch onto this shit*, she realized while calling LeLe.

Bellda still had no clue that she was sleeping with her ex's invisible enemy. And Pat had no clue that the nigga who had brought wrath on his and Black's establishment with regulation and slaughter was sleeping with his mistress, Bellda.

"Girl, pick up!" Bellda said impatiently while listening to LeLe's phone ring.

"Hello," LeLe breathlessly snatched up the phone.

"Damn, bitch! What's wrong with you?" Bellda asked.

"Bitch! None of yours. What do you want?" LeLe inquired.

Bellda had quickly put two and two together and concluded that she had stumbled upon the aftermath of her girl getting her morning groove on with T-Gutta.

"Keep on and y'all gone bare more than y'all can spare," Bellda retorted, getting a chuckle out of LeLe.

"Girl, what do you want?"

"I need some help. What should I cook Real this morning? Help me, and I'll bring you a plate."

"Bacon, fried eggs, sausage, cheesy grits, and some good-ass toast," LeLe fired off before Bellda could finish.

Fat bitch! Bellda thought of her friend.

"That do sound good!" Bellda said.

"Good, then cook it, 'cause, bitch, I'm hungry. All T-Gutta did was fuck me good and haul ass like always."

"Bitch, that's you and T-Gutta's problem!" Bellda said as she hung up the phone hearing LeLe laughing hysterically.

Bellda then began to prepare her man a delicious breakfast to be served in bed while playing Keshia Cole on her iPhone's Pandora playlist.

* * *

Despite the better scenery, Gina was missing Shamoney to the extreme. They hadn't communicated since the day Pat had cut him off. Every time she stared into her newborn's eyes, she saw Shamoney's striking resemblance. It only took Gina three months to realize that Pat was definitely not the father of Patron Jr. Pat himself was too engrossed in the streets to espy the small giveaway. Patron had Shamoney's eyes and adorable smile.

Lord, what am I gonna do if Pat questions me for whatever reasons? Gina asked herself while breastfeeding baby Pat.

Looking at her iPhone, she was tempted to call Shamoney and inform him of their creation. But she couldn't. She loved Pat too much to give away their location. She was aware of their beef, and she knew that Shamoney would kill Pat if he found him anywhere in the world.

Lord, how can two men be a part of me and be at each other's throats? Gina contemplated.

When Gina saw that Shamoney's swimsuit model wife was pregnant with twins, she was upset. She desperately wanted to ruin their happiness, since she yearned for happiness from Pat, who had been so busy running from his enemies rather than attending to his family.

I gotta get out of here before I end up in a fucked-up position, with no money and a dead husband, Gina thought of her future.

"I can't let him kill Pat. Lord, please help me," Gina cried out, softly wiping away her tears with her free hand.

* * *

"Yo, Kentucky. Check me out. Hit the track with me," Chucky said to Kentucky, who was about to hop in the long-ass canteen line.

Kentucky looked at the line and then quickly and logically weighed his options.

Fuck it! I'll catch it when it gets shorter, he thought.

It had been three months since the murder investigation was cleared, and he had been released back to open population on the compound. Within one week of being released, Kentucky had stabbed to death the lookout man from when he killed Jason—Jason's lookout man.

Kentucky and Chucky were still meeting up every day conversing about getting the fuck away from Martin Correctional.

"What's good, Chucky?" Kentucky asked as he proceeded to walk the track with Chucky.

Chucky furtively lit up a miniature kush blunt and passed it to Kentucky, who took a pull.

"It's the new shit, homie. Just hit last night. We have a pound of it," Chucky informed while holding in the smoke for an intense high, before he exhaled.

"Anything from the work camp?" Kentucky asked as he subsequently took a long pull on the blunt.

He was inquiring about the niggas who copped from him across the street where the low-custody inmates were housed. They were the ones who were permitted to work cleaning detail in the neighborhood, and they were one of the routes used to smuggle drugs into the prison.

"Yeah, they want in on half," Chucky informed Kentucky.

"Shit, as long as they got the money, then I'll handle the rest," Kentucky retorted.

"That's exactly what I needed to hear. Listen, I don't know if Real told you or not, but I need you to slow down on locking the compound down," Chucky told Kentucky, who was stabbing inmates every other week for the smallest things a person could do to tick him off.

Two weeks ago he had stabbed a man to death behind the chow hall for skipping him in line, and for the man calling him a pussy-ass cracker when Kentucky had confronted him. Everyone on the compound knew that Kentucky was no soft white boy and that he was not to be disrespected or underestimated. But the cat was naive.

"Man, I try to chill, but—"

"Listen, Kentucky," Chucky cut him off and abruptly stopped on the track, "I don't care how much iron you lay in a muthafucka. Shit, I'm with you. But I only ask this, homie, because our time is approaching real soon," Chuck concisely explained to Kentucky.

He didn't need to further elaborate for Kentucky to understand what he was conveying. Kentucky was able to fathom well.

"Is that so?" Kentucky said, passing the roach from the kush blunt to Chucky.

"Soon," Chucky reminded him, with an impish smirk on his face. "Soon, Kentucky! Like real soon!"

* * *

Johnny was at the 17th Street corner store in Ft. Pierce waiting for Su'Rabbit to come out of the store from macking with a bad-ass redbone bitch. While he was sitting in the driver's seat engrossed in his iPhone, car brakes came to an abrupt stop, which prompted him to look up. When he did so, he saw the Haitian nigga with a Haitian flag bandana around his face hanging out the passenger window of a money-green Explorer, aiming an AK-47 at his windshield.

Damn it! Johnny thought, ducking on time as the rapid bullets tore out his windshield to his new smoke-gray Tahoe truck on twenty-eight-inch rims.

He was caught slipping and had no clue how to evade the fusillade. Johnny retrieved his MAC-11 from beneath the driver's seat as the AK-47 continued to remodel his truck.

Chop! Chop! Chop! Chop!

When Johnny saw that the passenger door was getting hit up, he decided to take his chances and evade from the driver's seat. As he escaped the gunfire, he heard the distinctive sound of Su'Rabbit's earth-quaking .44 Bulldog.

Su'Rabbit had hit the gunman clean in his forehead, and continued to round off at the fleeing Explorer. The gunman's body fell from the passenger window and out into the street in the middle of the intersection on Avenue D.

Despite the many witnesses in the daylight, Su'Rabbit ran up the lifeless gunman and pumped more slugs into his body.

Boom! Boom! Boom!

It wasn't long before Johnny's bullet-riddled truck had pulled up alongside him.

"Nigga, let's go!" Johnny screamed, snapping Su'Rabbit out of his killer trance.

Su' quickly hopped into the truck, and they made it safely away from the scene.

"Nigga, yo' ass crazy!" Johnny said while laughing as he accelerated through the hood in Ft. Pierce on Avenue I en route to North 29th Street.

"No, nigga! That Zoe was stupid fo' thinking he was going to end my nigga day today," Su' exclaimed with high adrenaline.

"These muthafuckas would never get that lucky, my nigga!" Johnny confidently exclaimed. "Chyna Man too much fo' these niggas!"

Chapter Eighteen

When Real and Shamoney pulled up to the Holiday Inn in Palm Beach County, they both meticulously checked their surroundings like always. Real parked the black SUV next to a smoke-gray Suburban.

"Shit! Looks good, brah!" Shamoney gingerly said watching all dark cuts.

Real reached in the backseat and retrieved two black Nike duffel bags full of their re-up money.

"Well, let's do this, nigga!" Real said as he emerged from the SUV and quickly hopped into the backseat of the Suburban.

"How is me amigo?" Pablo asked Real while puffing on a Cuban cigar.

"I'm good, Pablo. Just taking shit slow and enjoying the good life," Real retorted, adjusting his Chicago Bulls cap.

In the front seat sat two of Pablo's bodyguards, who were ruthless Mexicans.

"That's wonderful. Is this for me?" Pablo asked, grabbing the two duffel bags from Real's lap and tossing them in the back, without any assurance from Real.

Pablo then pulled two more duffel bags from under his seat that contained twenty kilos a piece, and handed them over to Real.

"Have you spoken with Chucky lately?" Pablo asked.

"Yes, I did, Pablo. Chucky is on his way home," Real explained with a smile on his face.

"I knew that I could count on you, amigo. Anything you need, you let Pablo know, okay?" he spoke as he released a thick cloud of cigar smoke in the air.

Now is the time! Real thought.

"Pablo?" Real began, but paused while pulling on his goatee.

"What is it, amigo?"

"I know that you are aware of me and my men at war with the Haitian mafia, the same Haitians that Zo'pound is at war with too. I want to know, do you have any dealings with either of them?"

"Why? What's the problem, amigo? Spit it out like a hot burrito," Pablo retorted.

"The problem is me and my men gonna continue to hold our shit down. And if Zo'pound is in head with you, then I need to speak to the head nigga!" Real explained, followed by a moment of silence before Pablo spoke.

"Listen, amigo. You go at war with a lion's heart, and it's brave. But you must be careful. These men are very dangerous. I couldn't care less for the Haitian mafia, who are the same ones you are at war with. They're at war with everybody!" Pablo said with his hands. "Black thinks he's God and he can't be touched, amigo, but he is wrong," Pablo said, releasing another cloud of smoke. "I know Polo well, just like I know you, catch me?"

Real nodded his head in assent. "Yeah, I catch you."

"Polo does his own thing, amigo. For many years he's been hunting Black."

"Ask him, if I bring him Black or Pat, what's in it for me?" Real fired off.

Real knew everything about Polo and Black's beef from Shamoney. Putting him up on game, Real felt that two niggas gunning at the same enemy would prevail easily if they came together.

"I will ask that question of Polo and get back with you, Real," Pablo promised.

"Thanks, Pablo."

"No, gracias to you, amigo!"

* * *

It was 1:00 a.m. when V-Money saw Real pull up to Jake's store. He was sitting in his conspicuous lime-green Chevy Caprice on twenty-eight-inch rims, receiving good head from Pimp. He was grateful for the dark tints on the windows, or else he and Pimp would have been busted.

"Ease up, ma! I gotta go handle something," V-Money informed Pimp, who had increased her pace because she desperately wanted to bring V-Money to his load.

"Mmm!" Pimp moaned as she intensified her superb head game.

V-Money had his team getting the cash by all means. He was the lieutenant in the swamp. When the drop arrived, he was the first one to distribute it.

"Come on, ma. I'ma be back," V-Money said, just as he felt himself about to come. He let Pimp have her way and said, "Fuck it! Eat that dick, baby!"

Pimp moaned out to V-Money as she sucked him fast and deep.

"Shit!" V-Money exhaled in ecstasy as he exploded in Pimp's mouth, who sucked up every ounce of his load down her gullet.

"Girl, you a mess!" V-Money said, quickly refastening his belt and then hurrying from the car into Jake's store.

No nigga! You a messa! Pimp thought as she lit up a phat kush blunt and then exhaled a ring of smoke.

She felt good about herself after pleasing her sugar daddy and would wait on him to return to get the rest of the package.

That's right, nigga. I'm waiting on that good-ass tongue, Pimp thought.

Just the thought of how good V-Money would eat her pussy made her sultry and moist between her legs. She didn't care how long it would take him to handle business. It was all worth the wait.

V-Money found Real at the counter inside Jake's store, rubbing on Keshia's phat succulent ass.

Trifling-ass bitch! V-Money thought.

Real had no clue that Keshia and Jake had been creeping around since Joc's death, but V-Money knew well.

"What's good, homie?" Real asked V-Money as he dapped him up.

"Shit! Just waiting on you, brah," V-Money retorted while shooting Keshia a sour-ass mean mug.

Nigga, fuck you too! Keshia thought, rolling her eyes at V-Money before she stormed around Real, who grabbed her by the wrist.

"Where you heading at?" Real asked.

"I'm on my way home, boy. What's up, and why you grabbing me like you own me?" Keshia asked Real while simultaneously watching Jake to see what defense of a sugar daddy he had to present for her.

"Shit! Let me own you for the night!"

Before Keshia could slap the shit out of Real, he caught her hand with his free one and then twisted her wrist and placed her arm behind her back.

"Aww! Real, stop it! You hurtin' me!" she howled in pain.

"Who you think you're about to put your hands on, huh?" Real asked between clenched teeth.

"Sorry, Real. Pleeeese!"

Real released his grip and then pushed her away toward the door, staring at her with an impish look.

"When you quit playin' games, I'll be ready. Until then, get the fuck out of my face before I embarrass yo' ass," Real promised.

Keshia looked at Jake with tears in her eyes; however, he didn't stand up for her like she expected.

Nigga, you fucking me every night and you gonna let him handle me like this? Keshia thought angrily as tears cascaded down her face.

That's all she needed to see, because at that moment, she decided to make Jake pay in the most horrible way. Before she could explode, Keshia stormed out of the store. She was grateful that Jake had an all-wooden screen door, or else folks on the outside would have seen Real manhandle her. Her cries were drowned by the loud Jamaican music playing from V-Money's stereo resting on the freezer outside.

"I got somethin' fo' that lil nigga and Jake's ass!" Keshia said as she hopped into her purple Dodge Caravan and sped away.

"What the fuck is that bitch's problem?" Bruna said to his lil roll dawg, Phat Whinny, who had Okeechobee hood on lock and submissive to his regulation.

Phat Whinny was from the swamp and was about his issue on any given day.

"That bitch been actin' crazy since Joc left," Bruna said.

"Shit! Ain't Jake smashing that shit now?" Phat Whiny asked.

"Damn! That shit way in 'Chobee, huh?" Bruna asked.

"Man, you know I ain't missin' shit!" Phat Winy exclaimed.

* * *

The FBI in Miami had surrounded the Ramada Inn with a takedown unit. They were tipped off on Jean Pierre's (a.k.a. Black's) whereabouts in upstairs room 324. They moved quickly and furtively in their raid gear. In their hands were AR-15s in the ready position.

"Alpha, we're moving. Delta, prepare!" FBI agent Ted Davis said into his earpiece.

He was a lead agent and had been hunting Black for ten years yet always coming up short, even when he had Black in sight. Tonight he was determined to kill Black on sight and hold justice in the streets.

"Delta, copy!" agent Mike Stanley, Davis's partner, responded from the ground floor.

Davis was a brawny six foot four, 225-pound, solid, gray-haired white man who had been in the field for twenty years taking down some of the deadliest serial killers and drugs lords. His partner of fifteen years, Stanley, was a stubby five eight and 245-pound veteran as well, who had been with the FBI for twenty years. Neither of them had plans to retire until Jean Black Pierre was killed or brought into custody.

When Agent Davis made it to room 324, he halted his twelve men and then waved in his battering ram agents to their positions. The lights were on in the room, and vague yet gleeful female voices could be heard.

This is too good to be true! Agent Davis thought as he prepared to raid.

In his hands were two M84 flashbang grenades.

"Delta 2042, ready?" Davis said into his earpiece as he waited for the power to shut down in the room.

"What the fuck!" a woman exclaimed as the lights went out.

Agent Davis gave his men the go ahead, and quick as a finger snap, two brawny six foot five, 225-pound agents rammed down the door to room 324.

"FBI! Get down!" Agent Davis shouted, then tossed M84 flashbang grenades into the room.

Boom! Boom!

The strippers howled hysterically as they were thrown to the ground and roughly restrained. When the lights came on, Davis had his AR-15 aimed at his suspect.

"Kiss my ass!" Davis shouted in frustration and rage.

The man he had his AR-15 trained on was not who he had come for. It was a fiasco, and Davis was devastated while staring at the Haitian who strongly resembled Black.

Agent Davis lost his cool and fired on the man sitting nude in the chair with his hands up. He hit the man thirty times before he finally bridled himself and walked from the room, once again with negative results of apprehending or killing Jean Black Pierre.

"Suspect down at attempts to fire at agents," Agent Davis said into his earpiece. "Negative on Jean Pierre," he continued.

He could only imagine the look on his partner's face downstairs.

Chapter Nineteen

Real and T-Gutta were sitting in the trap house cooking up half of the product that they had gotten from Pablo while three naked hood bitches bagged up the dope in ounces and cut twenty piece-sized crack rocks. They were in the swamp where Real had six traps houses that were bringing in tremendous sums of cash. The dramatic change was definitely hurting the Haitian mafia, because everyone on the Treasure Coast in the tri-county area was fucking with Real and his brothers. He was also fucking with some Zo'pound niggas in Fort Lauderdale who were putting the buzz in niggas' ears from Miami about the 20.5 a kilo. Like Real had planned, he had circled the dope game and was now feeding the land honey and not peanuts like Black.

Every man was their own in his eyes. He had his restricted blocks that he strictly prohibited anyone from hustling on other than his own hustlers. That prohibited block was a small section in Stuart called Monterey. The section in Monterey was a constant twenty-four-hour strip, where the money came in every hour like traffic.

"Do Capo and Trap Money still want the two bricks?" Real asked T-Gutta about the two ruthless niggas who were holding down a hood in Hobe Sound, located in the west on the way out of Martin County.

"Capo wants to meet up after he comes back from visiting his brother, Juvie. He goes to see his brother every week at the prison. I told him a day or we'll be ready," T-Gutta explained.

"Go ahead and let them get them two," Real permitted while pointing at two cooked kilos of cocaine sitting on the counter in the kitchen.

When Real looked up into the dining area, he caught one of the female workers at the table named Bree all in his mouth, something that Real deeply hated.

"Bitch, why you all in my mouth?" Real exploded while storming out of the kitchen and toward the dining table, scaring the rest of the workers with his sudden outburst.

Bree was a petite redbone in her mid-thirties. When Real snatched her ass out of her chair by her throat, she wiggled and desperately tried to free herself from the death grip around her neck.

"You see me talking. Stay out of my mouth, bitch. Yo' job is to get this shit bagged and weighed, not look in my mouth, bitch! Do you understand me?" Real angrily asked of Bree.

Bree was unable to speak and could only manage a small head nod in assent. Her girls had warned her about her wandering eyes, especially in a nigga's trap house. Neither of her two coworkers, who'd know her their entire life, bothered to look up in pity, since they were afraid of being the next example.

Niggas are skeptical about any crazy movement, and being nosy is the cardinal mistake any bitch can make in this business, one of Bree's coworkers, Jessica, thought, as did their other friend, Jada.

That bitch is too nosy, and she gonna get herself killed! Jada thought as she and Jessica continued to work while their girl, Bree, was getting the shit choked out of her.

"Are we sure this won't happen again, bitch?" Real asked Bree.

Like before, she was only able to manage a head nod. Real hadn't realized that he had her almost a foot off the ground, until he let go of her and she collapsed to the deck.

"Sorry, it won't happen again, Real!" Bree exclaimed breathlessly while holding onto her throat.

Real looked at Bree with an impish smirk on his face. "I know it won't, or else next time you'll never come back to tell me so, I promise," Real said while looking down at Bree, who still held onto her throat with both hands while absentmindedly spreading her legs and exposing her shaven phat pussy.

T-Gutta watched Real from the kitchen with a smile on his face. He loved seeing Real check a nigga or bitch. Real had taught T-Gutta how to regulate the game and still make hos and niggas respect a nigga.

"Gutta, I'ma be back in a couple hours. Close shop at ten o'clock, fam," Real said as he left the trap house to handle business down in Fort Lauderdale.

* * *

Lala was throwing her daughter, Destiny, her third birthday party in the swamp at the community park. The other kids were from three to six years old and enjoying the waterslide and water gun war. DJ Train was keeping the music going for the grown and sexy while Birdman regulated the grill with his delicious barbecue ribs and chicken. Birdman was an old-school, stubby, oil-toned brother who didn't play when it came to barbecue.

For the past few months since her and Real's break-up, Lala had been solo, making a tremendous profit from credit card scams with her other Ms. Gorgeouses. She had no time for a man. Despite her ill will toward Real leaving her for another bitch, she remained calm and respectful when she was around him or randomly saw him around. When she heard from Pimp, who heard from V-Money, what Real had done to Keshia inside Jake's store, Lala laughed her ass off to the point of tears and pissing herself. She could only imagine how Real made that ho holla for mercy.

Damn! I miss my nigga fo' real. How the fuck am I out here letting another bitch play wifey with him? That's supposed to be me, Lala thought while watching Destiny have a splendid time playing with the other kids.

"Girl, there you go! What the hell is on your mind?" Mookie asked Lala while passing her a phat purple haze blunt.

"I'm thinking 'bout goin' to get my nigga back by all means," Lala said, taking a pull from the blunt and then exhaling. "You down or what?"

"Bitch, you sound crazy. Hell! I ain't down with no 187. That ain't got shit to do with ripping off Uncle Sam!" Mookie retorted, getting a laugh out of Lala.

It was just the two of them chilling underneath the pavilion away from the kids and adults who didn't smoke at all.

"Girl, I miss him," Lala purred.

Mookie wasn't trying to hear that shit. Her mind instantly went back to the good time she had with Real in Palm Beach at her hotel.

I think I need to call that nigga myself, Mookie thought.

"What you think I should do?" Lala asked, watching Pimp and Nut-Nut race up the sidewalk squirting the kids with their water machine guns.

"I think you need to let Real do him, and you do you. I mean, who could stop any dog from roaming other than the dog pound?" Mookie stated.

True, but that's my nigga! Lala adamantly thought, not wanting to hear what Mookie was telling her.

"I guess," Lala nonchalantly said as she stormed off to go play with Destiny.

"See, bitch, that's your problem now. You can't accept advice!" Mookie shouted.

"Whatever!" Lala said over her shoulder.

The moment Lala picked up Destiny from the sandbox, she heard shots erupt, sending everyone at the park into an uproar while trying to protect their kids and themselves.

Chop! Chop! Chop!

"Nooo! Please, God!" Lala screamed over the frenzied cries and shots as she lay on top of Destiny and the other small children in the sandbox.

The shots continued to ring out, hitting kids and adults. When Lala looked up, she saw the black SUV doing the drive-by shooting with the gunman hanging out the passenger window. She saw the Haitian flag bandana around his face and ski mask. He was nailing everyone who was moving and scrambling for their lives.

DJ Train was able to ward off the attack with his AK-47 rifle, but he had no luck at hitting the gunman, who had ducked back into the black SUV.

When DJ Train tried to pursue the SUV, he collapsed. He had been unaware at first that he had been hit, because of his high adrenaline rush. "I'm hit!" DJ Train howled in pain and panic while holding onto his bloody thigh.

Lala was grateful to hear Destiny's cries underneath her in the sand, and that none of the other kids in the sandbox were harmed either. When she sat up and saw the grieving mothers crying over their lifeless children, Lala broke down and tightly embraced her daughter.

Thank God she's safe, Lord, Lala thought.

"Noo, Nut-Nut! Lord, no!" Lala heard the shrill of Pimp.

When she looked behind her, Lala saw Pimp embracing a bloody bullet-riddled Nut-Nut against the restroom door. Lala stared into Nut-Nut's eyes and saw that she wasn't blinking. She knew death when she saw it, and she was now looking at it in her homegirl's lifeless stare.

"Noo! Nut-Nut!" Lala screamed as she made a dash over to her with Destiny in her arms. Before she could get to her, Birdman stopped her and abruptly took Destiny out of her arms.

"Don't take that child there, Lala. I got her," Birdman exclaimed as he held onto Destiny, who instantly calmed down her cries at the comfort of Birdman.

Lala and her remaining clique all embraced and cried over Nut-Nut, whose eyes were still open and not blinking with any sign of life.

* * *

When B-Zoe and his two lil niggas made it across the tracks to the Rimes food market, the trio quickly and furtively hopped out of the SUV and got into B-Zoe's black Charger. They had no run-ins with the multitude of Martin County sheriffs who were responding to the scene that they had just left bloody, unregretfully. B-Zoe then merged into traffic and traveled on the Bee Line Highway all the way southwest into Palm Beach County, where he then proceeded north back to St. Lucie County.

The long way home is always the safest at times such as now, B-Zoe thought, satisfied in his work. He was going hard for T-Zoe and had just made a grave mistake.

* * *

Meeting Polo was like meeting President Obama to Real. Like he had promised, Pablo made it possible for two of Black's enemies to come together. Polo liked everything about Real as a person thus far. He saw a very determined lion on the hunt for the same prey. He now had to see the heart of the man. He knew that when two lions cornered the same prey, they often took down the prey together. However, some lions then go at each other's throats. Despite liking the lil nigga's demeanor, Polo still had to figure out Real.

They were riding through the city limits of East Lauderdale in Polo's luxurious Hummer HZ. It was armored like all his other vehicles. Polo had shown Real his $4.5 million mansion out in Hollywood. He was now taking him on a tour through his hoods and introducing him to high-ranked Zo'pound affiliates. They were nothing like the Haitian mafia other than all being from the same country of Haiti.

"We have no understanding of the Haitian mafia, Real," Polo spoke. "Every night we take a dozen of them to show who rules the streets. We're nothing like Black, who thinks he can control the world to his liking. The FBI wants him because they have evidence on him, and I want him because it's personal," Polo explained while looking at his gold Rolex out of habit. "Many folks are afraid of Black, and I believe the FBI is too. I agree that Black is a powerful man, but you may be too young to understand my meaning of powerful. He is wise with his sacrifices."

What the hell is this man talking about? Real wanted to know. Unbeknownst to Real, Polo was hitting him with some deep shit.

"He'll never move like us Zo'pound, Real," Polo explained, before looking at his Rolex again and then into

Real's eyes. "If we wanted to regulate anywhere, then we could, including Martin County, which you've successfully taken out of Black's hands."

"You see, Real," Polo said as he passed a phat hydro blunt to Real, "it's easy to snatch something from the hands of a man who's afraid to show his face, but to find him is the real victory!"

"Why is it so hard to find him?" Real asked.

Good man! Polo thought, knowing that he had a real lion in his presence. *To ask a man of his weakness is to be for him, and to disregard is to plot against him,* Polo thought retrospectively of the words of his mentor—Black himself.

"Deep as I may want to go at him myself," Polo said, fondling with the black beads around his neck, "da gods will not allow either of us to kill one another."

Voodoo! Real thought. "So where is he?" Real asked. "I'll kill him and Pat. I can't find Pat, but I bet when I do, I'll find Black," Real retorted.

"You do dat, and I will make you into a very powerful man give you a forever pact with Zo'pound," Polo exclaimed. "And when I say powerful, I mean a millionaire, lil man," Polo added.

Real looked at Polo for a moment and considered what the man was telling him. He needed a strong alliance.

"I will do my end. Just be true on your end," Real said.

"Zo'pound will never have a bad name, Real. What Polo says, goes!" he promised.

Real knew of one way to get to Pat like a lightning bolt, and he had been contemplating the move for a while now. But in order for his plan to play out, he needed one person to assent to the plan and be down for the play.

The two lions continued to converse and learn about each other while riding around Fort Lauderdale, until Real turned on his phone and saw the very disturbing text from Shamoney: "Someone just hit the swamp. Kids they didn't spare. Complete mayhem!"

There were more texts from V-Money, Var, T-Gutta, Lunatic, and Ham all saying the same thing but in different words.

When Real looked at the time of the text, he saw that Shamoney had texted him at 1:45 p.m. It was now 8:00 p.m.

Damn! I can't believe this shit!

"Something wrong, Real?" Polo asked, after seeing the frustration on Real's face as evidenced by his corrugated forehead.

"Yeah, I need to get back. Black just killed some innocent kids," Real explained.

"Haitians, get us back in a hurry," Polo ordered his men.

When they arrived at a place Real didn't recognize, he became perplexed. He knew that it wasn't Polo's mansion. Before he could inquire, Real's back door opened, and a muscular, oil-toned, six foot five, 210-pound Haitian greeted him.

"Hurry! Come!" he barked while vigorously yanking Real by his arm and out of the Hummer's backseat.

The Haitian held a death grip on Real's arm and ran with him in an open field to an awaiting helicopter.

Get da fuck out of here! Real thought as he was pushed inside and nimbly secured by the Haitian man.

"Indiantown, Florida. Land in the field by the park!" the Haitian man barked at the pilot in Creole.

All Real understood from the Creole language was Indiantown, Florida.

* * *

"Man, I'm landing at the park. Dat's me, brah!" Real shouted to Shamoney over his iPhone as the Haitian descended the Bell helicopter in the middle of the soccer field.

"Brah, you don't see all these crackers out here!" Shamoney exclaimed.

"Man, fuck these crackers. They in the wrong place, not me, and dis our shit, Money!" Real retorted as he hung up on his brother.

Every officer and detective on the scene had their eyes glued to the helicopter. Some thought it was the FBI, while others expected to see the president step out.

"Who the fuck is this?" Det. Harris asked his partner, Det. Holmes while watching the man dressed in a business suit get off the helicopter and run up to a crowd of grieving folks.

"Whoever it is, they seem to know him well," Holmes retorted, then looked over at her partner, who was taking long strides to see who the big shot was.

She decided to let him handle whatever it was that he was on to, and continue her investigation of the crime scene where five little kids and six adults lay slain.

"Excuse me, sir. May I ask you a few questions?" Det. Harris asked Real, who was embracing his auntie Ms. Pig, who was crying for the loss of one of her grandkids.

When Real looked at the detective with a cold stare, Det. Harris quickly and instantly made out his features.

"Lil' Robbase, huh?" Det. Harris exclaimed, calling Real's father's name out.

"What you want to ask me? Why I'm jumping out a helicopter, or are you more concerned on finding the people who did this shit?" Real exclaimed.

"Sure! Could we have a talk at the station to affirm your whereabouts?" Harris sassily said.

"Nigga, you must be trippin'. You don't need to know my whereabouts 'cause I ain't did shit!"

"Then you should have no problem coming down to the station, Mr. Jermaine Wilkins," Harris retorted sternly.

"Sure, I'll come down," Real retorted, impishly.

"Very well, son. Let's go then," Harris said as he gestured with his arm and pointed with his index finger at his unmarked car for Real to lead the way.

"I'll be back, Auntie," Real said as he walked off with the Det. Harris, who met up with Holmes, who went along with the play without question.

She knew that Harris had found his first man to interrogate and pump for information. But unbeknownst to either of them, Real wouldn't speak to either without the presence of his attorney.

Ducks get plucked, and lions get respected, Real thought with a smirk on his face as he rode in the backseat of the unmarked Yukon and didn't say a word.

Chapter Twenty

"Pat, since when we start killin' kids, man?" Black shouted through the receiver of the phone.

Black was devastated when he heard the news that had occurred in Indiantown. This was the shit that made him hot, and enticed the FBI to sniff the ground with everything they had until they found the man behind the Haitian mafia. Despite killing kids in his past to offer them as a sacrifice to his gods, Black was against any random kids being slaughtered.

"Man, I didn't order that hit, man," Pat retorted back to Black in Creole.

Black was cruising through the city limits of Miami, being chauffeured around by his two Haitian bodyguards.

"What do you mean, the hit wasn't us? Is that what you're tellin' me?" Black asked. *Lie, nigga. Lie to me!* Black thought. "Look, Pat. We're moving backward, son. Our streets have been taken from us like we're some bitches. I can't come out to show my face, which means I'm counting on one muthafucka to control the land. Martin is our fuckin' gold mine, and some lil jitt just muscled it from us! What the fuck is goin' on, Pat?" Black angrily exclaimed.

"You want to know what's goin' on, Black?" Pat calmly retorted.

Black didn't like the tone in Pat's voice at all. He immediately sensed a sardonic remark on the way.

"We let loose a fuckin' animal, Black! Shamoney is a fuckin' animal, and his clique is worse!" Pat exploded angrily.

He's weak! Black thought of Pat, a man he had known never to back down to a nigga's wrath.

"So Shamoney is an animal, huh?" Black asked.

"An animal that we should have never cut loose," Pat reminded Black.

"Pat, what do you do to stop an animal?" Black asked. For a moment, the line went silent before Black retorted, "You go at his house hole, kill everything, stop runnin' from him, and start chasing him," Black ordered.

Speak fo' yourself! Pat thought, before promising, "I got you, Black."

* * *

When Pat got off the phone with Black, he made love to his wife, Gina, but he had Bellda in the core of his mind. He missed her, but he understood why she was avoiding him. He couldn't blame her actions, because she had warned him that she wasn't about to continue playing mistress. He saw her new man on Facebook, never realizing that he was staring at the man who had taken over his and Black's gold mine.

Pat had a lot of shit roaming through his mind. He seriously wanted to leave the game alone and live a normal life. He had enough money to retire and take care of three generations of his family. He and Black had become millionaires together—through drudgery.

Killin' kids was definitely not part of the script, Pat thought. *I gotta do something about it.*

Until then, Pat planned to use B-Zoe as his strength to complete the mission he now had planned. Lying to Black about not knowing who the assassin was did not get past Black.

Looking at Gina asleep after fucking her into a coma state, Pat emerged from bed and put on some Polo briefs. He then walked into his newborn's room. Patron Jr. was sleeping on his stomach. He was proud to bring a son to his life, after having three girls, none of whom were older than five.

But looking at Patron Jr. in his crib, Pat saw a soldier and the creation of an animal that his grimy wife pushed into this world. Pat knew all about Gina's infidelity and her affair with Shamoney. He also knew there was a strong possibility that Patron Jr. was not his. He had planned on killing Gina and Shamoney in the act. He was just waiting for the day Shamoney showed his face in Naples, knowing that Gina would lure him to their home. But he had underestimated Gina. She was being faithful and not risking any relations with Shamoney thus far.

"I got you now, soldier. We gonna really see how much of an animal you are, and see how much you love your creation," Pat said while softly rubbing his son on his back.

Suddenly, Pat vigorously snatched Patron Jr. from out of his sleep and shook him two times.

"Look at me in my eyes, lil man," Pat whispered in a shout.

When Patron Jr. opened his eyes, and didn't cry, Pat smiled at the soldier's solidarity.

"You a bad muthafucka, huh?" Pat said to Patron, who closed his eyes and drifted back off to sleep.

I know you are, Pat thought.

* * *

"Uhh shit, baby!" Bellda moaned out loudly as Real deeply thrust into her phat wet mound from behind.

The pleasure he was giving her had her in ecstasy and on cloud nine. In the background emanating from hidden surround-system speakers was "Bottoms Up" by Trey Songz and Nicki Minaj.

"Yes, dad. Damn! Beat this pussy!" Bellda purred loudly.

It was Bellda's day off from work and the beginning of her two-week vacation. Real promised to get away from all the mayhem in the city, so he had taken Bellda on a three-day trip to Kingston, Jamaica. They would return to Martin the day of the funerals for Nut-Nut and his lil cousin Tim, who were the last of the eleven slain at Indiantown Community Park to be buried.

Bellda knew that her man was going through a rough time, and she knew what to do to get his head to some level of sanity before he lost it.

"This pussy good, daddy?" Bellda moaned while she threw her pussy back into Real's strokes.

They were both sweaty and sticky from hours of love making.

"Answer me, baby! Is this pussy good?" Bellda demanded while coming to an orgasm.

Smack!

Real slapped Bellda's ass at the peak of exploding.

"Yes, baby! This pussy good!" Real grunted as he released an electrifying load inside of her for the fifth time that night.

"Damn!" he exhaled, letting himself drain into her womb.

"I love you, Jermaine!" Bellda purred while looking back at Real with the traditional sexy cat eyes of her culture.

"I love you too, beautiful," Real replied as he then collapsed next to Bellda, who climbed on top of him and lay on his sweaty chest.

She listened to his heart beat rapidly and thought what her life would be like if that heart that belonged to her suddenly stopped pumping. The thought made her tear up and reflect on what was going on in the city—their city.

Two counties not even an hour apart from each other are killing one another, for what? Bellda thought as the tears fell down her face.

Real knew Bellda, and he could tell she was crying, as evidenced by the shaking of her body. "Baby, what's wrong?" he asked.

Bellda wiped her eyes and then propped up on her hands under her chin on Real's nicely toned chest.

"I'm afraid, Jermaine!" she said as she sat up, straddling Real while looking into his eyes.

"Afraid of what, baby?" Real asked her.

"Too much killing on a little-ass coast, for what?" Bellda sniveled.

"Come here," Real said as he sat up and held Bellda in his warming embrace. "Baby, we gonna be alright. Daddy coming home every night."

"How can you be so sure, Real?"

"Because I know. We came here to ease our minds, baby, not to stress 'bout what's goin' on back home," Real reminded her.

"Yeah, but guess what? We still have to go back home, and the same shit will be occurring," she said, with her hands rested on both hips.

She has a point, but I live for bloodshed, he wanted to inform his concerned woman. "Bellda, one day it will stop, and there's nothing that me or your tears can do 'bout it, bae. I just lost a cousin and homegirl, and until I find the nigga responsible, baby, I'm droppin' at least three every night."

How 'bout I just give you the nigga myself. I'll set him up. But that means I'll have to come clean about holding Pat back from the start, Bellda thought.

"Baby, listen. When kids' lives were taken, it became a bloody mayhem. Two things that'll never sit well with me are a police killin' a nigga, and a nigga killin' an innocent child," Real explained, holding up two fingers.

"I can assure you that daddy will be home every night. I love you, Bellda, and one night without you is hell. That's why I'm home every night for you to wake up in the morning and see me by your side."

Before Real could utter another world, Bellda planted her lips to his and kissed him deeply. His sweet words had hit home and were comforting to her heart. One night without him would be hell for her as well, and Bellda couldn't imagine seeing that day ever come.

She badly wanted to tell Real where to find Pat, knowing that she could lure him into a death trap. But she knew that the war wouldn't cease at Pat's death. There was more to the Haitian mafia than Pat; she was sure of that.

Bellda began planting kisses down Real's still sweaty body until she got to his erect dick. Standing at attention again, she placed him in the confines of her mouth and slowly gave him head, which caused him to moan softly to her.

"Shit, baby!" he exhaled as she did tricks with her mouth.

Bellda swiftly reversed herself into a sixty-nine position and put her pussy in Real's face. Real parted her milky pussy lips and sucked on her pearl and asshole until they both came together.

Deep down, Bellda wanted to tell Real about Pat, if only it could end the madness. But she knew that it wouldn't. For some reason, she felt that she was making a mistake by not giving up Pat. She tried to muster the courage for the sake of the kids who were killed, but the thought of conspiring to murder ate her conscience. She wasn't built to stomach the street life of death, drugs, and blood money, where murder came behind betrayal. She was still loyal to Pat despite moving on from him.

I can't! Bellda thought as she continued to please her man.

Chapter Twenty-One

On the day of the funerals, Shamoney had tried numerous times to reach Gina, but to no avail.

"She's avoiding me, brah, on every corner," Shamoney said to Real.

They were both at Shamoney's mansion on the back patio, standing while staring at the thirty-foot pool. They were waiting for Chantele to put her final touch on Bellda's delicate curls with the hot iron.

"Do you think she's busy or around him?" Real asked, knocking off lint from his all-black, tailored Armani suit.

"I don't know, brah. I won't be able to tell until she picks up. Maybe we'll try later. I just was trying to handle this shit, before you and Bellda came back," Shamoney exclaimed with frustration.

"Don't worry yourself, lil brah. Everything will pan out," Real said, giving Shamoney a squeeze on his shoulders.

"I guess, brah!" Shamoney retorted.

After Real had enlightened Shamoney about the plan, to which he quickly assented, he had to get to Pat. Gina was just a piece of pussy to him, and now she would be the bait to lure Pat into their death trap. Neither brother would ever expect for the bullet that they were trying to shoot to backfire on them and become a fiasco.

* * *

Gina so desperately wanted to answer Shamoney's call, but she couldn't. She thoroughly missed him—his smile, tender touch, and sweet loving that he had given her. She was feeding Patron Jr. a bottle and watching the girls play in the enormous den. She had no clue where Pat had wandered off to, but she was sure that he would be in tonight. Ever since they had moved to Naples, Pat was home more than he had been when they were living in Lake Worth. She loved and missed Palm Beach, but she had to stick and move with her man.

I wonder how Shamoney is doing, though? Gina thought as her mind flashed to memories of them together. She would sneak around in hotel rooms with him while Pat was out of town, as well as sit up all night talking with him on the phone. There were a couple times when she and Shamoney would even make love in the same bed that she shared with Pat.

Damn! How can I be so trifling? Gina asked herself as regretful tears cascaded down her face.

"Mami, why are you crying?" her five-year-old daughter, Hatti, asked.

"I'm okay. Mami's just tired. When you yawn good, sometimes tears fall from your eyes," Gina covered up as she demonstrated a yawn to her daughter.

"Oh, so you're not sad!" Hatti asked her mother, still acting a bit concerned.

Gina smiled at her daughter, who strongly resembled her father, robbing her of any hint of Gina being her mother.

"No, baby. Mami's not sad," Gina retorted with a convincing smile.

After the kids, had tired themselves out, Gina fed them lunch and lay them down for a noon nap. When she walked over to her massive living room window, she stared out at the dark, overcast sky and saw that it was promising another downpour.

Her iPhone rang, blasting her Beyoncé's "Formation" ringtone. She knew it had to be Pat calling to check in. But when she saw the unknown yet familiar number, she knew that it was Shamoney again. And like every other one of his calls, Gina hit the side button and sent him to voicemail.

"I can't, Shamoney. I wish I could, but I can't. Now is not the time," Gina said to herself.

* * *

Chop! Chop! Chop! Chop! Chop!

The Haitians on 14th Street in Fort Pierce were taken off guard by the deadly fusillade from Su'Rabbit's AK-47 as he hung out the window. There were five of them, and he artistically nailed all of them.

"Stop the car!" Su' told Johnny, who was navigating the stolen Dodge truck.

Johnny abruptly stopped, and Su'Rabbit jumped out like a mad man, nailing more Haitians who were coming out of the targeted trap. Johnny hopped out with his AR-15 and went to work on his feeble, defenseless foes, bringing the count to eleven dead Zoes.

"Let's go, brah!" Johnny yelled.

When he turned around to head back to the truck, he was startled when he saw two unmarked Yukons and two detectives aiming their M-16 rifles at him and Su'Rabbit.

Shit! Johnny thought.

"Put down the weapon now!" the detectives demanded.

The world was moving slowly for Johnny. He was caught, and the wrong fart would have him sleeping for eternity. Johnny slowly lowered his weapon, afraid of being killed, but before he could place it on the ground, Su'Rabbit exploded.

"I can't go out like this!" Su'Rabbit shouted as he opened up on the two Yukons while simultaneously making a dash to the side of the Haitian's trap house.

Luckily, he wasn't hit by the gunfire that followed. The detectives were focused on Su'Rabbit that they had forgotten about Johnny.

Now or never! Johnny thought.

"May luck save my day!" Johnny said as he came up with his AR-15 and caught both detectives head first and off guard.

When they both dropped to their deaths, Su'Rabbit ran from the side of the house and hopped in the truck with Johnny.

"Good job, Chyna Man," Su' exclaimed as Johnny accelerated and left the scene.

Bending a corner at the same time, backup had arrived from behind. Fortunately, backup had missed the Dodge truck and was only left with two dead detectives and eleven slain Haitian mafia Zoes.

* * *

On 10th Street in Ft. Pierce, Lunatic and T-Gutta successfully ran into a Haitian store and left five dead employees, including the manager, while also removing video tapes and robbing the safe. The outburst of slaughter had everyone on guard and afraid to step out of their homes. Police were everywhere hunting down the perpetrators, to no avail.

"I bet these muthafuckas get their mind right now!" Lunatic exclaimed to T-Gutta, who was gingerly watching the road for police while he carefully maneuvered through traffic on their way back to Martin County.

"Brah! Johnny and them whacked the five-oh (police). This shit 'bout to be super hot!" T-Gutta said while looking at the breaking news in St. Lucie County.

"Fuck the police! They shouldn't have brought their ass to the scene. Since when us swamp niggas ever spare shit?" Lunatic exclaimed.

"You have a point, dirty!" T-Gutta retorted.

* * *

"Breaking news in St. Lucie County in the city of Ft. Pierce, where two horrible murder scenes have taken place, both around 5:00 p.m. today, leaving a total of nineteen dead. Among the death toll are two Ft. Pierce major crime detectives who responded to the scene on the 2100 block known as 14th Street.

"This is the worst scene that's occurred within the murder-rated county. And once again, we have no clues or cooperating witnesses to either scene. 14th Street is known for high crime, and this is believed to be in retaliation from other gang rivals of the Haitians who are at war among themselves.

"The horrible scenery on the 3100 block known as 10th Street also seems to be connected. If there's anybody who could lead us to these perpetrators, please call our hot tips line at 1-800-855-TIPS or 1-800-855-3432.

"It is important that we get justice for these victims, and get the killers off the streets. My name is Rebecca Smalls, and I'm live on 14th Street, reporting for your local Channel 12 News," the black reporter in her early twenties said.

Black was again furious after watching the news update. The murders had hit worldwide and had now received state emergency attention, where President Obama was giving a sympathetic speech to the families of the slain victims. Further, he ordered the FBI to step in and gain control of the mayhem along the Treasure Coast.

"This isn't good, Pat! Not one bit, son!" Black said to himself in the confines of his low-key palace in Naples.

The last thing Black needed was for the FBI to get involved, because it wasn't like they were just hunting him. Now they had an opportunity to break down every Haitian in order to get to him.

It's times like this when I feel like I'm on borrowed time, Black thought as he rubbed the stress from his eyes and lay back on his comfortable bed.

He then closed his eyes in prayer, hoping that it was all a dream and not a bloody mayhem down South.

* * *

Lunatic and Ham were getting back from a club in Miami. They were both wasted and were grateful that they had made it back to the swamp without any run-ins with the law. Lil' Boosie emanated from the speakers of Lunatic's Mercury at a low volume so as not to attract any attention to them. As they navigated through the hood on Fox Road, they saw Keshia's purple Dodge Caravan in the park's lot next to a black Explorer.

"Wonder who that ho tricking with now?" Lunatic said to Ham as they passed the park and were both attentive to Keshia's business.

Neither of them recognized the Explorer, and it wasn't Jake, who everyone knew had recently been hitting on her.

"I dunno who da fuck dat is!" Ham exclaimed.

When they passed Jake's store, Lunatic saw V-Money and a couple of his soldiers still out trapping. It was three o'clock, and the block was still in action.

"Man, run me to the crib, brah. I'm takin' it in for the night," Ham told Lunatic, who pulled up to the store.

"I'll be right back. Gotta grab me a beer," Lunatic told Ham.

When he got out of the Mercury on twenty-five-inch rims, he dapped up V-Money and his lil brother, A.J., who was trapping like every other nigga at the store.

When Ham looked further down the road, he saw the black Explorer he had seen at the park pull off a corner. He then saw Keshia's van coming towards Jake's. He watched Keshia pull along the side of the store and then walk in from a back door. It was definitely no secret that Jake was fucking Keshia, since she even had her own keys to the store. A moment later, Lunatic emerged from the store with a Budweiser inside a brown paper bag.

"Alright. I'll fuck wit' you niggas later. Be careful!" Lunatic said to all the niggas trapping as he got into his Mercury and peeled off.

"Yo! Something fishy 'bout that ho Keshia," Ham stated, not knowing why he felt that way.

"Man, it's always something up with her. She just like da rest of these hos fuckin' for a dollar," Lunatic exclaimed while turning onto Ham's street.

"Nigga, I should have made yo' ass walk from Jake's store. I'm wastin' my damn gas!" Lunatic said to Ham, who only lived two blocks away.

"And it would have taken me two days to get here," Ham retorted as he got out of the car.

Boom! Boom! Boom! Boom!

"That sounds like Jake's!" Lunatic said, putting the gear into drive when he took off.

Ham was halfway in the car, fumbling with closing the door. When Lunatic made it to the corner, he and Ham saw the black Explorer at Jake's store. Two masked men were laying down the whole store, including Phat Whinny, who took two slugs. Lunatic sat at the corner and killed his headlights and then reached under the driver's seat to retrieve his two Glock .40s. Ham was already in action and didn't need to be told anything.

When the gunmen's backs were turned, Lunatic gently tapped on the gas pedal and allowed the car to roll over to the intersecting street to 5th Street. Once across, he quickly accelerated onto the next street. When he got in front of two apartments stationed behind Jake's store, which shared the same gate, he killed the engine and got on foot with Ham, avoiding taking the gate.

Lunatic and Ham then sprinted on foot circulating the block until they came to the corner and saw both masked gunmen pulling V-Money by his dreadlocks with a gun to his head. One of them kept a close eye on all the niggas who were laid down, as well as Jake's front door, for any heroes. The gunmen struck V-Money in his temple, knocking him out cold, and tossed him in the backseat of the Explorer. They then hopped inside while the other men made a dash for the driver's door, but they were nailed by Lunatic's Glock .40s.

Boom! Boom! Boom!

The gunman inside quickly panicked and tried climbing to the driver's seat to flee, but he was hit by the bullets smashing through the windshield, driver's window, and back window.

Phat Whinny was wearing a bulletproof vest, which obviously saved his life. Once he no longer heard gunfire, he sat up and joined Lunatic and Ham. All three then rounded off inside the Explorer, airing out the gunman. When Lunatic ran up to the Explorer, he saw the gunman down. It didn't take him a second to know that he was dead, but he still pumped two more slugs into his face.

Boom! Boom!

Lunatic then pulled out V-Money from the backseat while Ham ran inside Jake's store.

"That ho Keshia set this up!" Lunatic informed Phat Whinny and V-Money.

Lunatic looked around and saw that three of his homies were laid out dead as well. He was grateful that neither of them was his lil brother A.J., who had run from the store when he saw the gunmen first pull up.

Inside the store, Ham looked around and saw no signs of Jake or Keshia. The television was at a high volume, blasting ESPN, just like always. With his Glock 21 in hand, Ham walked toward the back of the store and down the dimly lit hallway. He discovered the back door wide open.

She tryin' to run, Ham thought, almost moving on that idea, until he made it to the poorly lit restroom.

Inside, he found Jake sitting on the toilet with his pants down and a blood stain in the middle of his white Polo shirt, in the center of his chest. His eyes were wide open. The blood trickling down the side of his mouth proved to be game over for Jake.

"No, man!" Ham exclaimed while shaking his head from side to side in disbelief as he absentmindedly walked further inside the restroom, unaware of Keshia standing behind the restroom door.

Ham heard the click from the hammer of a .357 being pulled back. It startled him, and he instantly turned around with his gun raised. He saw Keshia standing there with tears cascading down her face and a .357 shoved in her mouth. Before Ham could squeeze his gun, Keshia pulled the trigger.

Boom!

"Bitch!" Ham shouted as Keshia's brains exploded out the back of her head and onto the filthy restroom walls.

Ham couldn't believe that she had taken her own life along with Jake's. Ham then aimed at her body and squeezed his Glock smoking empty while tears flooded his face. He then exited the gruesome restroom and out the back door to relay the shocking news to Lunatic and V-Money.

* * *

When Lala received the news of what was occurring at Jake's store, she rolled out of bed with a still-sleeping Birdman next to her and quickly punched in Real's phone number to see if he was alright. She knew how close Real was to Jake, and he'd be one of the few taking his death real hard. She was worried despite them no longer being together. He would always be someone special to her.

She had been seeing Birdman since the day her girl Nut-Nut was killed. Birdman inevitably grew on her, since he was there to console her and help her look after Destiny. She was lonesome and needed the affection Birdman was giving her. He was old-school at forty-five years old, and he knew how to cater to a woman's every need and desire. She was grateful for him, but her heart still yearned for Real.

Lala got no answer from Real, after trying him three times in two minutes.

I hope he's alright, she thought, sitting on her sofa in her satin robe. *This is too much. I can't raise Destiny 'round here. I gotta relocate*, Lala thought while rubbing her temples, out of frustration. *Damn! I hope he's okay!* she thought again, trying his number one more time to no avail.

Chapter Twenty-Two

Two Weeks Later

Gina awoke from her sleep sweating from the stuffy atmosphere in the room, since the air conditioner had been cut off, which was highly unusual.

Why is it so damn hot in here, and where the hell is Pat? Gina wanted to know, after discovering that he was missing from the bed. *I wonder where the hell he's at?* Gina thought as she emerged nude from their king-sized bed and then slid into a pink satin robe.

Gina walked out of the room and downstairs, where she saw the illuminations from the mute flat-screen television lighting up the entire living room. When she saw, the images displaying on the TV, her heart dropped and began rapidly beating.

"Oh my God!" she exclaimed while staring at her and Shamoney wildly fucking on the same bed on which she and Pat made love and shared.

"Uhhh shit, daddy!" Gina's cries came off mute, which startled her and made her almost jump out of her skin.

When she turned around, she stared into the eyes of her husband, who had a devilish smirk on his face while holding a sleeping Patron Jr. in his arms.

"Pat, I'm sorry, baby. I'm so sorry that this happened."

"There's no need to be sorry, Gina," Pat said as he walked toward his wife, who began backing away from him fearfully.

The look in his eyes was a look she had never seen on him before. He had Patron Jr. in his arms, so she knew that he was aware that the baby wasn't his son.

"Eleven years, and you had everything from nothing, Gina!"

"I'm sorry!"

"I gave you the world, and you played me like a yank. What was it, Gina? Too much rope, huh? Or because yo' hero saved your day when I couldn't?" Pat inquired as he backed her into a corner.

"Pat, it was a mistake!" Gina cried while badly trembling. *He's going to kill me.* "Pat, give me a chance. I will give him away for adoption."

Smack!

"Agghh!" Gina cried out from Pat's backhanded slap that spun her around to clutch the wall for support. Blood trickled from her busted lip as a result of the rough slap.

"No, Gina. You're going to be a real mother and bring this baby to his father!" Pat demanded.

He wants me to set up Shamoney. Oh my God! Gina thought, afraid to turn around and face Pat.

He spun her around by her shoulder to face him.

"I'ma ask you again, Gina. You're goin' to bring this boy back to his daddy, right?"

Gina looked at Patron Jr. and saw that his eyes were now open as opposed to being closed when he was yawning a minute ago. She had to do whatever would suit her husband. She couldn't let him down any more than she'd already done, so she decided quickly. "Yes, Pat. I will bring him to his daddy," Gina responded shamefully while looking down at the ground.

"Go get dressed, and I mean hurry up!" Pat shouted.

"What about the girls, Pat?"

"The girls are fine. They're with their new nanny. Now do as I say, Gina," Pat demanded.

Gina quickly stormed around Pat and dashed upstairs.

A nanny? He's been planning this all for awhile, Gina concluded as she looked into the girls' empty rooms.

"Pat, please don't hurt our children," Gina cried out.

She badly feared for her kids and couldn't imagine seeing him harm them in any way. She had seen the compassionate way he cared for and played with them. The girls were his heart, but she had never seen the compassion he had for the girls given to Patron Jr.

"Oh my God. He's known since Patron Jr. was born that he wasn't his child," Gina said to herself while she got dressed and prepared to set up the real father.

* * *

Black now had all the pieces of the puzzle. He was not only at war with Shamoney, but also his eldest brother, who was most responsible for the sudden wrath.

Real, huh? Black thought while sitting in the backseat of the luxurious limo.

He was tired from running from the FBI and his enemies, especially those who didn't have the heart to face him like a man. Pat had given Black the information passed down from B-Zoe, who had lost two of his soldiers while trying to abduct one of Real's lieutenants.

Keshia is the one to thank, not Pat or B-Zoe, Black thought.

He would see that Real and Shamoney took their last breaths at his hands. It had been years since Black had had to lay down a nigga himself. He would not leave it to any other man to silence the two who had his gold mine in their palms.

He was disappointed in Gina for her infidelity, but he also thanked her, because if it wasn't for her sleeping with the enemy, he wouldn't be in the position to have his enemies in his reach. Now all that needed to happen was for Shamoney to walk into the trap.

What man would deny their own blood? Black thought.

Once Shamoney and Real were gone, Black would give his sacrifice to the gods, a sacrifice for which the gods themselves had asked and one that would restore him the power to regain his lost gold mine.

* * *

Since Real had buried his mentor, Jake, he had been on the edge and was on a slaughtering spree. Bellda did everything in her womanly power to keep her man sane and with a comforting place to dwell in with her. She knew that Real was out killing muthafuckas, as evidenced by the blood on his clothes. She just played it cool and prayed that he was careful and would come home to her every night.

They were enjoying the pleasure of each other while relaxing in their Jacuzzi. Bellda straddled Real with her arms around his neck and slowly rode his dick. She was making love to him and wanted him to know that she was there for him. She understood his grief, and she made it her business to console him thoroughly.

"I love you, Jermaine!" she purred as she felt herself on the edge of her orgasm.

"I love you too!"

"Uhh shit!" Bellda released, with her body trembling from the electrifying orgasm.

"Arrghh!" Real grunted while exploding inside her. "Damn, baby. I love you!" Real exhaled as he passionately kissed Bellda.

After making love to her, Real showered with his woman, made love to her again, and then prepared himself for the task he had in front of him.

It was 4:00 a.m. when Real stepped out the front door in his all-black attire. Bellda watched him leave in his smoke-gray Suburban, with an eerie feeling in her stomach.

"Something about to go down. Today just don't feel right. Lord, please watch over my baby," Bellda prayed, and then walked back into their bedroom, where Real's scent perpetually lingered.

She cuddled in bed with his pillow until she fell into a coma-like sleep.

* * *

"Delta Zone, one line up for breakfast. Last call!" the sergeant announced over the loud PA system.

It was 5:45 a.m. and they were the third dorm called for morning chow.

Kentucky hopped out of his bottom bunk after playing possum on his cellmate. For years he'd routinely gotten up every morning precisely at 4:00 a.m. to do his hygiene, make his bunk military style, and then lay back down on top of his made bunk awaiting the chow call.

Kentucky's cellmate, Ronnie, who was a new arrival, hopped down out of his top bunk and began his super-fast hygiene. Kentucky walked past him and out of the cell to line up with the other inmates.

"Last call. Last call. File out!" the sergeant exclaimed as he popped open the front door to allow everyone to file out into the sally port.

"Hurry up, snail!" the sergeant shouted to Kentucky's cellmate, Ronnie, who was running as fast as he could.

Ronnie was a tall slim redhead and looked like his knees were climbing his chest at every stride he took. He was the only one lacking a jacket and would surely pay for it once winter hit.

This kid better get with the program, or he's gonna have a long thirty years, Kentucky thought as he looked at his G-Shock digital watch and saw that it was now 5:49 a.m. *Hurry, man!* Kentucky thought.

He had to be behind B-dorm with Chucky at 6:15 sharp.

When Ronnie made it to the door and breathlessly closed it behind him, the sergeant popped the sally port door and allowed the eighty-two inmates to file out into the dark morning atmosphere. It was foggy, and the watch towers had the spotlight illuminating the cold darkness.

Kentucky looked at the two watch towers and knew that behind the spotlights were two trained COs in each tower armed with M-16 rifles. The sun wouldn't come up until 6:45 a.m.

Kentucky saw the darkness as all game. He had stabbed plenty of enemies in the confines of morning darkness and left them for dead.

When he passed C-dorm, he saw the inmates gathered in their own sally port about to be let out to file off to the chow hall as well. Kentucky furtively began dropping back in line to catch up with Chucky, who would be coming out of C-dorm. Because he had his hands in his jacket pocket, the veteran inmates knew that Kentucky was up to something. And they knew when he was about to stab one of his enemies.

Chucky was the third inmate in line and stormed out of C-dorm with his hands buried in his jacket pocket as well. It was in the low forties in the winter, a season that Chucky loved, for it reminded him of his childhood growing up in New York.

"What's up, homie?" Chucky spoke to Kentucky as they continued to the chow hall.

"I can feel it in my veins," Kentucky retorted.

"Tell me 'bout it. I stayed up all night on coffee."

"Hurry along, inmates," CO Raff yelled at the group coming through the north chow hall gate standing next to his captain.

"I swear I want to stick 'im," Chucky mumbled under his breath.

He hated Raff with a passion.

"Stick 'im then!" Kentucky enticed Chucky.

"Shit, I just might do that, homie!" Chucky retorted with an impish smirk on his face.

Kentucky knew beyond a doubt that Chucky would stick CO Raff without hesitation.

"Only problem I see, you'll have to get to him before I do," Kentucky said as they walked into the chow hall.

It was quiet as the COs walked the aisles barking out orders.

"Table four, last row. Hurry up and get out of my mess hall!" a sergeant named Taylor barked at the inmates in the last row out of five.

Talking was seriously prohibited in the chow hall. It was strictly eat like a hog in a three-minute cycle, look out for your enemies, and get the fuck out of Dodge.

It was "shit on the shank" day, a breakfast consisting of grits, gravy, mystery meat, biscuits that weren't worth coming for, and bad potatoes. Kentucky and Chucky grabbed their trays from the slot behind the brick wall and seated themselves at the third table in the second row. They both gave away their trays and waited until their row was called.

It was 6:12 a.m. when Chucky checked his G-Shock digital watch, identical to Kentucky's, while filing out of the exit door. COs wore gloves while randomly frisking inmates. Kentucky and Chucky both sighed when they passed the COs.

At 6:14 the two heard the blades of helicopters, and their stomachs instantly formed butterflies. When the spotlight trained on the approaching Bell helicopters, Kentucky and Chucky made a run for B-dorm. The both of them ran together with their shanks drawn.

"Hey, inmates! Come here!" CO Raff shouted while running after the duo with two other COs as four Bell helicopters circled the prison.

"Get them fuckers out of here now!" Captain Johnson demanded on his walkie-talkie.

The gunmen in the towers were perplexed and had no idea what was happening. They fired at the circulating helicopters, which initiated into a fusillade; however, they missed each one. One of the helicopters circled the towers and fired an M28 rocket launcher at each tower, taking out every CO inside.

"Holy mother!" Captain Johnson screamed and then ran for cover.

When Chucky and Kentucky made it to the back of B-dorm, Chucky grabbed the wall with Kentucky and stuck his shank into CO Raff's larynx, dropping him quickly as he came around the corner. Kentucky took out the other CO, striking him through his temple. The last bold CO dropped his radio and attempted to flee the danger. But he stumbled, and both Kentucky and Chucky stabbed him on both sides of his neck, and left the fourteen-inch shanks in his neck, piercing through both sides.

When they saw, the helicopter circle the center of the field and drop a lengthy heavy-duty rope, Kentucky and Chucky made a dash toward it and began climbing, until they both entered the bed of the helicopter with the Haitians from Zo'pound.

The helicopters then parted together. Kentucky and Chucky had covered the mile distance to the swamp in no time. The prison guards and authorities were confused and had no clue which helicopter to pursue, after the helicopters split north, east, west, and south.

When Chucky and Kentucky's helicopter descended in the soccer field at the community park in the swamp, Kentucky could see the flickering headlights on an SUV. The helicopter landed, and both men ran toward the SUV and hopped into the backseat, where they both met Real, who was grilling his mouth full of golds at them.

"Didn't I tell y'all niggas I was comin'? Real niggas do real things. Shamoney, meet the realest cracka you'll ever meet, and Chico too. Chucky and Kentucky, this is my lil brother, Shamoney," Real introduced everyone and then got the fuck out of Martin County.

The authorities were chasing two escapees in helicopters, not on the ground. The Haitians were professionals who Martin County authorities were not prepared for and certainly not equipped to take down. They got away like the professionals they were, leaving a bloody scene behind and torching the ground with the M28 rocket launcher like they were flying dragons.

Chapter Twenty-Three

It was eight o'clock when Real and Shamoney made it to St. Lucie County after driving back from Tampa where they left Chucky and Kentucky with Pablo.

The FBI was ablaze in Martin County, with useless bloodhounds searching for the escapees—drudgery to no avail. The three-county manhunt for them went nationwide, with another state of emergency by the president.

Bellda and Chantele had called their men with the breaking news, including all their lieutenants, who knew nothing of the escape. Real had kept the plot strictly between him and Shamoney. He was grateful for Polo's assistance. Zo'pound had left a serious body count in Indiantown, between the sheriffs and innocent civilians traveling along Highway 710.

When Real pulled into the driveway of their mother's home, he and Shamoney saw their stepfather, Migerle, under the hood of his F-250 Ford pickup. He was happy to see them. It had been hell in Martin County, and he and their mother were worried sick about them.

"Well, how are you two?" Migerle spoke in a heavy Haitian accent. "Yo' mother is goin' crazy about you two's whereabouts."

"Her and the world, it seems," Real answered.

"I'd shake you boys' hand, but as you can see, I'm covered in oil," Migerle explained.

"Yeah, I see. What's the problem?" Shamoney inquired. At the same time he received a text alert on his phone.

"The starter went out on me, and a crack in my head," Migerle responded while Shamoney was engrossed reading the text.

"How 'bout we get you a new one?" Real recommended.

"It'd be nice, son, but you know I can't take no dirty money. We've been over this before," Migerle retorted, knowing that his stepsons got their money from selling drugs.

Neither Migerle nor their mother would accept a dime from them. However, before their mother became a devoted Christian, she'd never deny a penny.

Shamoney's silence prompted Real to look over at him. Real saw his odd facial expression as Shamoney read the lengthy text from Gina.

"Everything cool, Sha?"

Shamoney looked up at Real with locked jaws and an impish look on his face. Despite his anger displaying, he was still able to keep a cool head and demeanor.

"Yeah, let's see Mom. Then we have to go pick up Chantele," Shamoney played it off smoothly.

Real quickly picked up on the throw-off, knowing that Chantele, despite being prohibited from drinking, was at his palace with Bellda and LeLe having a girls night.

"Yeah, let's do that, brah," Real said as he walked inside with Shamoney to visit their mother, Michele, and baby sister, Precious.

* * *

"A baby boy that looks just like you, nigga. Damn, brah! You not even playin', and got a set of twins on the way!" Real exclaimed after looking at the text from Gina on Shamoney's iPhone.

The baby boy irrefutably had Shamoney's eyes and nose; neither of them could deny it. Beyond a doubt, their mother would have come to the same conclusion. Despite the picture, the text was skeptical. Gina had requested to see Shamoney at the Ramada Inn in Stuart, a motel where they had met on many occasions during their affair.

"It's your boy, lil brah, but it's a setup all day. I don't trust it," Real retorted.

They were sitting in Shamoney's living room contemplating their next move.

"I'ma call her, and then go off my better judgment."

"Our better judgment, when you tell me how you're going to approach. I'll tell you how I prefer to go about it," Real said.

Shamoney thought for a moment: *Real can smell enemy blood miles away. He feels it, too!*

"Okay, we'll check yours out too. But I'm calling her now," Shamoney declared as he dialed Gina's number.

Real called a redbone bitch named Trina, who worked the midnight shift serving room service.

The phone rang twice for Shamoney.

"Hello," Gina's voice spilled in his ears.

"You know who this is. So why so long to tell me this?" Shamoney asked Gina, getting straight to the point.

"I, I, I'm sorry, Shamoney," Gina broke down.

Thus far, things seem genuine, Shamoney thought.

"What room you in?" Shamoney asked.

"Room 200. I've been away from Pat."

"Why?"

"'Cause we got into it 'bout him always being gone. I didn't want to ruin my marriage. That's why I didn't answer any of your calls. It's been eatin' me keeping this from you, Shamoney. You don't have to claim him, but just know he's yours, and I want you to see him."

"Stop talkin' crazy, Gina. You know I'll take care of mine, so don't go there."

"I'm sorry, Shamoney. Please just come!" Gina cried.

"I'm comin'. I'll be there in an hour," Shamoney said.

"Promise?" Gina asked, testing his honesty.

"Promise," Shamoney said, followed by an eerie silence before Gina spoke again and concisely gave him the play.

"Okay, we'll be there," she said as she disconnected the call.

"He's there!" Shamoney informed Real, who had a smirk on his face. "I know he's waiting on us."

* * *

Smack!

"Agghh! Pat, please!" Gina cried out in pain after Pat vigorously slapped her the moment she had gotten off the phone with Shamoney, causing her to fly from the bed to the floor.

"Bitch, you love that nigga. You played a good game, you stupid bitch!" Pat shouted out to Gina before he kicked her in her stomach, causing her to ball up on the floor.

"Agghh! Please! I did it!" Gina cried in a roar.

"Bitch, give me that phone," Pat demanded through clenched teeth as he snatched the phone from Gina's trembling hands.

He then walked over to the motel's phone, snatched the cord from the wall, and disconnected the cord from the phone as Patron Jr. cried on the bed.

"Bitch, you will never do this again! I promise!" Pat said as he put the cord around Gina's neck and then began throttling her until she passed out.

When Pat saw that she was unconscious, he left the room, leaving Patron Jr. crying hysterically. He walked downstairs, out the door, and hopped in the backseat of a black Suburban with dark tint in the parking lot. The atmosphere was foggy from the purple haze smoke.

"So what's up?" Black asked, with a MAC-10 resting on his lap.

"He's on his way in an hour," Pat replied to Black.

"Good. Now we wait!" Black said, blowing a cloud of smoke.

Sitting up front were two of his bodyguards, who both had a striking resemblance to Black and were part of his sacrifice to the gods as well.

"Yeah, we wait!" Pat responded.

* * *

When Det. Harris received tips that something serious was about to occur at the Ramada Inn between some Haitian men and locals, he immediately passed the information on to the FBI. They were in town assisting Martin County in a three-county manhunt, searching for the two dangerous escapees.

"So tell me again, ma'am. You say that the Haitian man is indeed this man in this photo lineup?" Agent Davis asked the informer in the motel office.

"Yes, I'm positive. I can't forget those features," she explained.

"Can we review the tape?" Agent Stanley asked the informer's manager.

"Come this way," the manager directed the agents. He was a tall slim black man in his fifties. He advised his employee to call the authorities when she informed him of her firsthand knowledge.

When both FBI agents reviewed the tape and saw the Haitian man getting room 200, they both smiled brightly.

"I see why they call this tri-county area the Treasure Coast. Shit! Luck don't come no better than this," Agent Davis exclaimed while looking at the duplicate of Jean Black Pierre.

"You guys don't accept any more customers, and please call the surrounding rooms. Tell them to stay inside until further notice, for the sake of their own safety," Davis directed the manager.

"Send her home. We'll be in contact," Stanley said.

"Yes, sir," the manager answered as he then led Trina safely off the premises.

* * *

When Pat stormed back into the room, he found Gina on the bed feeding a bottle of milk to Patron Jr. Pat saw her split lip and closed eye, and he almost felt sympathy for her. But he couldn't show any empathy although deep down he still loved her.

Through their eleven years of marriage, he had never hurt her. So it was a first-time experience for them both. Something wasn't right, and there was only one way to find out.

"It's been over an hour. Call him and see what's taking him so long," Pat demanded as he threw the phone at Gina so she could call Shamoney.

With trembling hands, she called Shamoney's phone, which rang persistently with no answer. "He's not picking up!"

"Try again," Pat shouted while nonchalantly snatching Patron Jr. from her arms.

"Please, Pat. Don't hurt him!"

Smack!

Pat smacked Gina with all his force, which caused her head to smash into the headboard, which tremendously dazed her to the point that she was literally seeing innumerable stars.

Pat again snatched the phone from her hands.

"He has another hour or you'll die with him!" Pat threatened Gina, who didn't know what to think of the threat.

She watched Pat leave the room again, this time taking Patron Jr. with him.

"Please, Lord, don't let him kill my baby," Gina softly cried out as she began praying for the safety of herself and Patron Jr.

Pat has no compassion for Patron Jr., and that's dangerous for them both, Gina realized.

"It's my fault!" Gina cried.

I hope he remembers. Please remember, Shamoney, please! she thought as she broke down in hysterics.

Chapter Twenty-Four

Shamoney definitely did not miss the cryptic language from Gina.

"We'll be here!" was a clear understanding between them both that Pat was around. There was a moment of silence before she informed him.

That nigga around, Shamoney thought as he pulled into the Ramada Inn.

The revelation only confirmed Real's instincts, and once again, Real was five moves ahead of his enemies. His adrenaline was high, and he still was moving and meticulously planning. Real already had niggas moving in position standing on lookout. While Lunatic, T-Gutta, and Bruna were sitting in a Chevy Malibu, they saw when Pat exited the room. He had a baby in his arms, and then hopped into the backseat of the black Suburban.

Shamoney parked his Chevy Tahoe truck on the back side of the Ramada Inn. It was 11:45 p.m., and he thoroughly searched the scenery.

When he saw no threat, Shamoney emerged from the truck and then walked into the dark confines of the motel. When he walked past a soda machine, he saw an old white homeless man trying to keep warm.

Shamoney kept it moving, clutching his Glock .40 in his hands.

Click! Clack!

"Put your hands in the air and turn around slowly. No stupid shit! Let's not get yourself killed," FBI Agent Davis, who Shamoney had just taken for a homeless man, demanded.

Not wanting to test the waters, he slowly turned around with his hands in the air. He saw the homeless man aiming a

Glock 21 at him with one hand and his credentials in the other. "FBI agent Tod Davis."

"What the fuck!"

"And I'm FBI agent Mike Stanley," the other detective said as he artistically cuffed Shamoney after taking him by surprise.

"Let me guess, you're here to kill Black and probably Pat too, huh?" Agent Davis asked Shamoney while pulling the Glock from Shamoney's waist and inspecting it for a serial number that he knew he wouldn't find.

"No number. How many bodies?" Davis asked.

"Probably yo' mama and—"

"Agghh!" Shamoney shrilled when Davis punched him in the gut, silencing Shamoney after catching him with a TKO uppercut to his jaw line.

Shamoney's legs turned to jelly, but Stanley held him up. Stanley then tossed Shamoney over his shoulder and carried him inside room 52, which he and Davis were using as their temporary base.

* * *

Real was furious that Shamoney was not picking up the phone. When he pulled up to the Ramada Inn, he circled the entire perimeter and saw Shamoney's truck but not him.

"Where the fuck is he?" Real said to T-Gutta over his phone.

"We seen him come in, but we never saw him get out on his feet," T-Gutta explained.

Something isn't right. Real instinctively felt it deep in his gut.

* * *

Detectives Harris and Holmes watched Pat exit the Suburban again with the baby in his arms. There was something about the way he held the baby that made Holmes sense that he cared nothing for him. She had kids herself and knew when she saw a compassionate parent. This man didn't give a damn about the baby in his arms. And it irked Det. Holmes to see how nonchalant he was with the baby in the cold with no winter gear.

But this jackass is wearing a jacket, Holmes thought. "Something's not right with him and that baby," Holmes said to Harris.

They were positioned in the woods directly in front of room 200. The entire place was surrounded by undercover agents. Everyone saw it at once: the Suburban taillights illuminated and the engine started.

"He's leaving!" Holmes said into her walkie-talkie, informing Agent Davis. "Stay on them. Matter of fact, move in now!" Then "No! No! No! 10-54 disregard!" she exclaimed over the walkie-talkie when she saw Black step out of the Suburban and walk upstairs with Pat to the room. "He's secured inside room 200. A positive read," Holmes informed Davis.

"Ten-four, ten-four!" FBI Agent Davis replied, highly elated and eager to take down Black.

The Suburban pulled away, but no one bothered to pursue the SUV, since their eyes were on Black and Pat.

* * *

"Oh shit! Bitch, they raiding, brah. This shit is a trap!" T-Gutta shouted as he watched the innumerable FBI raid team creep upstairs.

"Say what, nigga?" Real asked in complete shock over his phone.

He was moments away from getting on foot to go look for Shamoney, until he heard T-Gutta. When Real circled the building, he too saw the raid team with M-16 rifles and shields.

"Damn! This shit is a trap. They gotta have Shamoney!" Real exclaimed, hitting the steering wheel. "Fall back. Man, get out of here!" Real told T-Gutta as he rammed his SUV into reverse. "I can't believe this shit, man!" Real said in complete disbelief, getting as far away from the motel as he could. "Trina!" he shouted, after quickly putting two and two together.

The bitch pulled a snake move, Real thought.

* * *

Shamoney couldn't believe how the FBI was everywhere. They had the place surrounded, and he had walked right into their trap.

But how the fuck did anybody know? Shamoney wanted to know.

He was left in the room with two other agents who weren't saying anything. They were only listening to the cracking of their radios and typing away on their laptops. Shamoney was clearly hearing the takedown of the legendary Black.

With his hands bound in cuffs behind his back, he couldn't do anything. It was irksome thinking of how he was going to escape from the custody of the FBI. They had the gun and most likely would arrest him for it like the agent had promised, along with conspiracy to murder their fugitive.

Damn it! How can life be such a bitch! Shamoney thought.

He knew the feds didn't play fair, and he couldn't outsmart them like they had done to him and his brother. He was about to become a father, and all he wanted was to be there for them. Now he had a son who he knew was his, yet he couldn't help him at the moment like he had intended. He had no choice but to sell his story to the FBI and pray that they would have sympathy while he prayed for the safe return of his son. As a man, he was going to own up and tell Chantele, and whether she respected him or not, he was not about to abandon his own blood.

* * *

FBI Agent Davis once again was leading the raid team to swiftly take down Jean Black Pierre and Patron "Pat" Sinclair, with AR-15s and M-16 rifles in their hands.

They slowly crept up to room 200. Per routine, Davis stopped short of the door as he carefully and instinctively listened. He heard the cries of the baby and said a silent prayer for his safety. Kicking down the door and not knowing where the baby was, was Davis's only fear.

He waved the two men operating the battering ram around him, and they stood prepared in front of the door.

"1652. All power now!" Davis said into his earpiece.

"Ten-four," the agent answered.

A second later, all power in the building was shut down.

Lord, here it goes! Davis thought.

Detectives Harris and Holmes watched the raid from a distance. The baby could be heard crying. At a finger snap from Davis, the door came down with the battering ram, followed by two M84 flashbang grenades.

Boom! Boom!

"FBI Agent, get—!"

Boom! Boom! Boom!

Before Davis could complete his orders, shots were fired. Pat first shot Gina and then turned his gun on the agents while Patron Jr. cried in his arms. Pat backed himself near the bathroom while squeezing his Glock .45.

When the lights came on, Davis had one clean shot, and he quickly took it, hitting Pat in his forehead; he immediately dropped with the crying baby.

Davis looked at Black and saw that again he had been tricked, as the man resembling Black lay on the floor, blind from the flashbang grenade. As other agents rescued the baby, Agent Davis shook his head in disbelief.

"Muthafucka!" Davis hysterically screamed as he emptied his clip into the man who everyone had mistaken for Jean Black Pierre.

* * *

"So tell me, B-Zoe, why the kids?" Big Chub asked.

Big Chub had come by himself, knocked on the front door, and taken B-Zoe's wife as a hostage. When B-Zoe looked up while sitting on the leather sofa in his living room watching football, he was surprised when he saw Chub with a gun to his wife's head. He attempted to go for his MAC-10 that was resting on the living room glass table. However, Chub popped him twice in his gut with this Glock .40 and then rocked B-Zoe's wife to sleep, squeezing two slugs into her head.

On the living room floor imbruing the snow-white carpet with the blood pouring from his gut, B-Zoe knew that he was on borrowed time until death came upon him. "Man, we family!" B-Zoe winced in devastating pain while crawling away from Big Chub, dragging his lower body.

"Kids, B-Zoe. All fo' what?" Chub asked again, referring to the kids that B-Zoe had killed in the swamp in the drive-by shooting.

The mafia was strongly against killing kids, and now B-Zoe was forced to pay drastically with his life.

"T-Zoe was family," B-Zoe said in pain. "What? We forgetting that they killed one of us?"

"No, B-Zoe. War got T-Zoe, not them kids. He was caught on the wrong side of the road. Just like you are now," Chub said as he aimed his Glock .40.

"For the deadly sin you've committed in the mafia's name. Taking the death of innocent kids is cardinal. We, the committee, feel that death should be sanctioned to you, B-Zoe."

"Fuck the committee, pussy-ass, nigga. Tell the maf—"

Boom! Boom! Boom! Boom!

Before B-Zoe could finish his disrespect toward the Haitian mafia, Big Chub emptied the clip into his face, leaving him deformed in a gruesome splatter of blood and brains.

Big Chub exited the opulent home in Killa County and inconspicuously left the scene.

Big Chub then took I-95 south all the way to Miami and met up with his Uncle Black, who had once again played five moves ahead of his enemies.

Epilogue

Two Weeks Later

After Shamoney explained that his purpose for being at the Ramada Inn was to save his son from a serial killer, the FBI believed his story, under the perilous circumstances, and freed him.

Despite a battered face, a bullet to her right shoulder, and a graze to her temple that left an ugly scar, Gina had survived by the grace of darkness.

"So, what are you goin' to do now?" Shamoney asked Gina, who was lying in the hospital bed with a bandage wrapped around her head and a sling on her right arm.

Shamoney was feeding Gina some delicious pecan ice cream and had been up to see her every day since her admission at St. Mary's Medical Center. However, due to the ongoing investigation and Black still being on the loose, today was their first visit.

"I'ma change his name, Shada," Gina responded.

"To what?" Shamoney asked curiously.

"To Shada Alexandra Wilkins."

"In other words, that's a Jr., lil brah," Real chimed in from the corner of the room.

He was sitting in a comfortable chair playing with this nephew, Patron Jr. Gina had put a warm smile on Shamoney's face.

I got me a Jr., Shamoney thought with elation.

"So, friends fo' life. No baby mama drama?" Gina retorted, stipulating their future relations.

"Yeah, friends fo' life," Shamoney agreed, giving Gina a pound on her good fist.

"How could I not be? You saved me twice," Gina almost choked.

"Real, thank you too. You came out of nowhere and made a difference in all our lives," she added.

"Blood is always first," Real said.

Gina could see Real talking, but could no longer hear him. When she looked at Shamoney, she saw that he was attentive to what Real was saying.

"Shamoney," Gina screamed, but she couldn't hear herself either.

What's going on? she thought as she began to panic.

When Gina looked toward the door, she saw a very dark-skinned doctor in his scrubs smiling at her.

Neither Shamoney nor Real was aware of the doctor standing in the doorway. But Gina's heart dropped when she recognized who he was.

Oh my God! Gina thought.

He smiled at her and then winked his eye.

"The gods will never let you get away with your infidelity. I gave Pat to the gods as a sacrifice for the sake of the kids. The gods only want everything you can hear," Black said to Gina as he stormed away from the room, leaving Gina deaf to all sounds on earth.

When she looked over at Real and Shamoney, they were laughing, and Patron Jr. was crying as Real tried his best to comfort him.

He put voodoo on me! Gina thought.

STAY TUNED FOR BOOK TWO

WARZONE

BOOKS BY GOOD2GO AUTHORS

GOOD 2 GO FILMS PRESENTS

THE HAND I WAS DEALT- FREE WEB SERIES
NOW AVAILABLE ON YOUTUBE!
YOUTUBE.COM/SILKWHITE212

SEASON TWO NOW AVAILABLE

To order books, please fill out the order form below:

To order films please go to www.good2gofilms.com

Name:_____

Address:_____

City: _____ State: _____ Zip Code: _____

Phone:_____

Email:_____

Method of Payment: Check   VISA   MASTERCARD

Credit Card#:_____

Name as it appears on card: _____

Signature: _____

Item Name	Price	Qty	Amount
48 Hours to Die – Silk White	$14.99		
A Hustler's Dream - Ernest Morris	$14.99		
A Hustler's Dream 2 - Ernest Morris	$14.99		
Business Is Business – Silk White	$14.99		
Business Is Business 2 – Silk White	$14.99		
Business Is Business 3 – Silk White	$14.99		
Childhood Sweethearts – Jacob Spears	$14.99		
Childhood Sweethearts 2 – Jacob Spears	$14.99		
Childhood Sweethearts 3 - Jacob Spears	$14.99		
Childhood Sweethearts 4 - Jacob Spears	$14.99		
Childhood Sweethearts 5 - Jacob Spears	$14.99		
Flipping Numbers – Ernest Morris	$14.99		
Flipping Numbers 2 – Ernest Morris	$14.99		
He Loves Me, He Loves You Not - Mychea	$14.99		
He Loves Me, He Loves You Not 2 - Mychea	$14.99		
He Loves Me, He Loves You Not 3 - Mychea	$14.99		
He Loves Me, He Loves You Not 4 – Mychea	$14.99		
He Loves Me, He Loves You Not 5 – Mychea	$14.99		
Lord of My Land – Jay Morrison	$14.99		
Lost and Turned Out – Ernest Morris	$14.99		
Married To Da Streets – Silk White	$14.99		
M.E.R.C. - Make Every Rep Count Health and Fitness	$14.99		
My Besties – Asia Hill	$14.99		
My Besties 2 – Asia Hill	$14.99		
My Besties 3 – Asia Hill	$14.99		
My Besties 4 – Asia Hill	$14.99		
My Boyfriend's Wife - Mychea	$14.99		
My Boyfriend's Wife 2 – Mychea	$14.99		
Naughty Housewives – Ernest Morris	$14.99		
Naughty Housewives 2 – Ernest Morris	$14.99		

Naughty Housewives 3 – Ernest Morris	$14.99		
Never Be The Same – Silk White	$14.99		
Stranded – Silk White	$14.99		
Slumped – Jason Brent	$14.99		
Tears of a Hustler - Silk White	$14.99		
Tears of a Hustler 2 - Silk White	$14.99		
Tears of a Hustler 3 - Silk White	$14.99		
Tears of a Hustler 4- Silk White	$14.99		
Tears of a Hustler 5 – Silk White	$14.99		
Tears of a Hustler 6 – Silk White	$14.99		
The Panty Ripper - Reality Way	$14.99		
The Panty Ripper 3 – Reality Way	$14.99		
The Solution – Jay Morrison	$14.99		
The Teflon Queen – Silk White	$14.99		
The Teflon Queen 2 – Silk White	$14.99		
The Teflon Queen 3 – Silk White	$14.99		
The Teflon Queen 4 – Silk White	$14.99		
The Teflon Queen 5 – Silk White	$14.99		
The Teflon Queen 6 - Silk White	$14.99		
The Vacation – Silk White	$14.99		
Tied To A Boss - J.L. Rose	$14.99		
Tied To A Boss 2 - J.L. Rose	$14.99		
Tied To A Boss 3 - J.L. Rose	$14.99		
Time Is Money - Silk White	$14.99		
Two Mask One Heart – Jacob Spears and Trayvon Jackson	$14.99		
Two Mask One Heart 2 – Jacob Spears and Trayvon Jackson	$14.99		
Two Mask One Heart 3 – Jacob Spears and Trayvon Jackson	$14.99		
Young Goonz – Reality Way	$14.99		
Subtotal:			
Tax:			
Shipping (Free) U.S. Media Mail:			
Total:			

Make Checks Payable To:
Good2Go Publishing
7311 W Glass Lane,
Laveen, AZ 85339